Red Rook

Midnight Empire: The Restoration, Book 2

Annabel Chase

Red Palm Press LLC

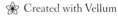

Chapter One

I couldn't believe the nerve of this monster.

"I'm not paying twenty dollars for a used suitcase," I insisted.

The seller splayed his arms. "Then I guess you'll be leaving your precious cargo behind because that's the going rate. They don't make 'em like this anymore."

I angled my head to admire the blue suitcase. The seller was right, damn him and his high-pressure tactics. The suitcase was the right height and sufficiently sturdy to accommodate some of my taller weapons and there was no way I was leaving them behind.

The seller jabbed a finger at George, who was perched on a nearby awning. "Throw in the baby dragon and I'll make it fifteen."

"The phoenix is not for sale. How about a banana?" I reached into my bag and produced the yellow fruit.

His gaze flicked to the banana, and I noticed his tongue dart out to swipe his lower lip. "Any other fruit?"

I thrust the offering forward, along with fifteen dollars.

"It's delicious potassium and fiber. What more do you need?"

"Deal." He took the banana and the cash, and let go of the suitcase, which immediately toppled over thanks to a bum wheel. I'd have to see if Liam could fix it before I left town.

The suitcase bumped along the sidewalk behind me as I dragged it back to my apartment. "Let that be a lesson to you, George. It pays to haggle."

The phoenix burped a response. I wasn't insulted. He did that a lot. I got the impression he suffered from some kind of acid reflux on account of the fire brewing inside him at all times.

We crossed Ninth Avenue and continued straight across midtown. It was only when we crossed Eighth that I realized I had a tail.

I drew to a stop. "Hey, George. Keep an eye on my suitcase."

The phoenix required no further explanation. He swooped down and landed on the handle, ready to take the purchase airborne if necessary.

I whipped around to confront my stalker. Grabbing him by the throat, I shoved him against the nearest wall. The move clearly took him by surprise. He wasn't even holding a weapon.

"There are dozens of women walking the streets at this hour and most of them don't have a miniature bodyguard. Why choose me?"

I took a good look at him. Under six feet, medium-build, hazel eyes. Pretty nondescript as far as stalkers went.

"I'm not here to attack you," he wheezed.

I squeezed harder. "You make a habit of sneaking up on

women and *don't* intend to attack them? You need a more productive hobby."

He made no move to defend himself. "Trinity Group sent me."

Trinity Group. Well, Olis warned me this would happen. The Director of Security for House August was also a wizard involved in a secret organization determined to bring back the sun.

I released my grip and took a step back. "Tell your people what I already told Olis—I'm not interested and I'm moving." I angled my head toward the suitcase. "Imminently."

He rubbed the tender part of his neck. "We want to invite you to attend a meeting."

"Then send a letter, not a stalker."

"You know we can't put anything in writing."

The mere existence of their group would be considered an act of treason. Restore the sun and you inevitably condemn vampires to the shadows once again. No more Houses. No more vampire rule, hence treason.

"I won't be here to attend any meetings. Sorry." I wasn't really sorry. I had no desire to get mixed up in species politics. I had my freedom now and I intended to make the most of it. What that entailed, I'd yet to decide.

"They'll consider you the enemy," he said.

"So I've been told." Olis had issued the same warning when he told me about the Trinity Group and his belief that I was a necessary part of their plan. I'd expressed the same level of interest then—zero. I'd spent my life taking orders from others, first as an assassin and then as an indentured servant. Now that I'd earned my freedom, I wasn't rushing to entangle myself with a group that wanted to use me as a weapon, which was essentially what the prophecy foretold.

"You're a witch. You should want this," he said.

"You don't know anything about me. You have no idea what I want."

What I wanted was a future I could never have, which was one of the reasons I'd decided to leave New York and create a life for myself elsewhere. New York was ruled by House August and House August was ruled by King Alaric. The vampire was...

No. I couldn't let my mind go there. We couldn't have the relationship we deserved. The king would have a rebellion on his hands if he chose a former killer of vampires as his queen. Yet I couldn't bear to stay here and watch him choose someone else, as he inevitably would. Leaving was the right thing to do for both of our sakes.

I grabbed the handle of the suitcase. "I'm heading back to my apartment now, where I will be planning the route to my new life. Please tell your friends I would be happy to attend their meeting, but, alas, I'll no longer be geographically desirable."

"They can be very persuasive," he said.

I leveled him with a look. "I promise I can be more so."

The expression on his face suggested he knew about my magic and didn't wish to be on the receiving end of it. Smart guy.

I turned away from him and continued the trek to my apartment. George hovered closer to me now, seemingly concerned that more Trinity Group members would climb out of the woodwork. I wasn't worried. I'd be gone by the time they sent their next recruiter.

I entered the apartment and gasped at the sight of a werewolf in my kitchen. "What the hell, Liam?"

My best friend held up a key. "I came by to return your spare key."

I propped the suitcase against the sofa. "Keep it. Maybe you'll hit it off with the new tenant."

"Doubtful." He gestured to the map spread across the small dining table. "Still deciding?"

"Yeah." I'd been looking at the map every day for two weeks in an effort to make a decision on where to go next. I couldn't bring myself to commit to a location. Too big. Too small. Too rural. Too cold. Too quiet. Nowhere was just right.

"You could swing past the Wasteland and check on Twila and the children."

"It's definitely on the list of options." The Wasteland was formerly known as Washington D.C., the nation's capital. After the Great Eruption, the area had been overtaken by monsters and an ambitious wizard until recently when my friends and I intervened.

"Have you heard from Meghan? Maybe you could crash with her, too."

"Haven't heard from her." Not that I expected to. I'd met the werewolf when she tried to avenge the murder of her husband, a vampire I'd been hired to kill. To the surprise of both of us, we became friends —sort of.

Liam rummaged through the meager contents of my fridge. "I know I've said this a hundred times, but you don't have to go."

"I know. It's a choice." I folded the map. "You should head out. I need to get ready." I'd foolishly agreed to one date with Alaric before I left the city. We'd settled on a Broadway production of *Romeo and Juliet*, mainly because it fit Alaric's hectic schedule.

Liam closed the refrigerator door holding a broken wedge of cheese. "I assume you're wearing the black dress."

"What else?" It was the only nice piece in my wardrobe thanks to Alaric. He'd bought the dress for me when we were involved the first time around. It fit like a glove, and I felt like another woman wearing it. Not a blood witch. Not a former assassin. Not a recently freed indentured servant.

Just Britt.

I loved that dress.

"Don't take any weapons," Liam advised. "They'll ruin the illusion."

"What illusion is that?"

"That you're the kind of woman who wears dresses and attends Broadway shows."

I snorted. "I'd give you my ticket, but Alaric might object."

"Object? He'd have me executed for interference with getting laid."

"I don't think that's a law."

Liam cast a forlorn look around the apartment and I knew he was contemplating a future without me. I knew because I was doing exactly the same thing.

"I'll let you get dressed," he finally said. "I want to hear all about the show tomorrow. I hear the vampire who plays Mercutio is hotter than a volcano."

"I'll try to take a picture for you. Do you have any plans tonight?"

"I'm meeting this guy PJ for a drink later."

"Wolf?"

He nodded. "I met him through a matchmaker that used to work in-house for one of the bigger packs."

"Sounds promising."

The werewolf shrugged. "I've learned to temper my expectations."

As he started toward the door, he attempted to slip the map under his shirt. I cleared my throat. Wordlessly, he returned the map to the table and left the apartment.

I hurried to change for the show. If this was the last night Alaric would see me for a long time, I wanted to look my best. I'd developed a sense of honor—but I also had an ego.

Once I was dressed, I peered into the oven where I kept a stash of weapons. Sighing, I closed the door. Liam was right. Weapons clashed with the dress. On the other hand, weapons were like my security blanket. I needed *something*. I opened the oven door and selected a 10-inch dagger. Hiking up my dress, I strapped the dagger in my garter. There. No one would be the wiser.

A knock on the door made my heart skip a beat. George wisely flew out the window to give us privacy.

"Coming, Your Majesty," I called in a singsong voice that sounded nothing like me. One dress and I was suddenly Snow White.

I yanked open the door to greet Alaric. His signature scent hit me first—grapefruit and frankincense. The vampire wore his medium-brown hair wavy and slightly disheveled. He looked more royal than usual in a charcoal suit with a red tie.

His mouth quirked as his green eyes raked over me. "I'm not sure I can handle you in a dress. I might want to..." The gold flecks in his eyes seemed to brighten. "I don't think you want to know."

"Tell me after the show."

"Actions speak louder than words." His gaze continued to linger on me in that predatory way that made me simultaneously want to flee and succumb. When his hand slid down my hip to the side of my thigh, I didn't object.

"What's this lump I feel?"

I smiled up at him. "Isn't that supposed to be my question?"

"Seriously, Britt. What is it? You know you can't bring a weapon into the theater. Security will notice and we're trying not to draw attention to ourselves."

I edged away from his hand. "It's only one little dagger. I can't leave them all at home. New York is a dangerous city."

"And you're a dangerous witch, or have you forgotten all your lovely nicknames?"

I hadn't forgotten. Death Bringer. Britt the Bloody. They were far from lovely, but they were accurate.

"It's for your protection," I said. In truth, it was out of habit—a habit I wasn't ready to break. Now wasn't the time to be complacent. I was about to venture into the big, wide world on my own. I had to shore up my defenses, not let my guard down.

Alaric leaned over and whispered my name. His lips brushed my earlobe, triggering a pleasant shiver. I was so caught up in the moment that I failed to object when he lifted my dress and liberated the dagger from its hiding spot. I was still relishing the feel of his hand on my bare skin when he held the blade in front of my face.

"*This* is prohibited in the theater."

"No, saying 'Macbeth' is prohibited in the theater. When they say, 'Is this a dagger I see before me...,' you can answer in the affirmative."

"We're seeing *Romeo and Juliet*."

I snatched the dagger from him and looked down at my

attire. "I can't put it back where it belongs without hiking up my dress."

He smirked. "I volunteer as tribute."

I glared at him while returning the dagger to its hiding spot. "Good thing I wore a garter." I hoped the sharp blade didn't poke me in the thigh the rest of the evening.

Alaric tilted his head to observe my legs. "I didn't realize you were wearing stockings."

"I'm not."

"Then why wear a garter?"

I offered a vague smile. "To give your fangs something to do later."

His eyes blazed with hunger. "How thoughtful."

"You have the tickets?"

He patted his jacket. "All set." He offered his arm. "Shall we?"

"Are you sure you want to do this? It's a public outing."

"You'll be pleased to know I haven't told anyone I'm attending, not even my security detail."

I wasn't sure 'pleased' was the right word, but I understood. I was the one who refused to attend his coronation ceremony because I didn't want to do anything that might undermine his authority. Royal vampires didn't have witches as consorts, and they certainly didn't have former indentured servants. As a mistress, yes, but not as an official partner.

"Olis won't be happy with you," I said.

"Olis is never happy." He adjusted his tie. "I'm incognito. What could go wrong?"

"You're a pretty recognizable figure. Don't you think they'll figure it out?"

"The only one who knows me well enough will be on stage. She's one of the stars."

"Let me guess. Ex-girlfriend."

He smirked. "Is there any other kind?"

I was tempted to punch his arm, but I resisted. Alaric was king now. I wasn't sure I could punch him even in jest without some goons toppling me.

As I locked the door, Liam emerged from his apartment down the hall. "Don't you look gorgeous," he remarked. "You look nice, too, Britt." The werewolf sauntered toward us. "Am I supposed to genuflect or does our shared history cancel out any formalities?"

Alaric looked down at him. "I suppose I'll overlook your transgression this once."

"Think of it this way, with me leaving town you'll probably never see each other again," I interjected.

"Stop saying that." The werewolf shot a pleading look at Alaric. "Can you command her to stop saying that? She's not going anywhere."

Alaric grunted. "As though I could command her to do anything."

Liam shook his head, disappointed. "Some king you are."

"Be careful what you wish for. If I were anything like my father, your head would already be on a spike for insolence."

King Maxwell's murder had been a shock to everyone. As a vampire, Alaric had believed he still had many years before his ascension to the throne. He hadn't felt ready to wear the mantle of responsibility. Ultimately, he had no choice. His mother, Queen Dionne, recognized her own inability to rule and passed the crown directly to Alaric.

Liam's gaze slid to me. "He's not like his father, right? We've established that."

I nodded. "Come see me tomorrow before I leave."

Liam walked toward the stairwell. "More lies," he called over his shoulder. "You're not going anywhere."

"He's going to be very sorry when he shows up in my empty apartment later this week," I muttered.

Alaric nudged me with his broad shoulder. "See? Nobody wants you to go. That means you should stay."

I looked up at him. "What about what I want? Does that not count?"

His expression softened. "Of course, it does. I didn't mean to suggest otherwise."

Granted, I wasn't experienced in making life choices. The major ones had been made for me.

As we exited the building, I noticed George circling above our heads in a frenetic fashion. "Buddy, this is a Broadway show. No animal companions allowed." I didn't catch the phoenix's response. I was too busy staring at the glowing red clouds gathered above him. "That's odd."

"What?" Alaric followed my gaze.

A gust of wind whipped past us, stirring up dust and debris on the sidewalk.

"Must be a storm front moving in," he observed.

I continued to stare at the strange sky. "Have you ever seen a storm with clouds that glowed red?"

"Don't tornados cause that?"

"I have no idea. When was the last time the city experienced a tornado?" The answer was not in our lifetime.

Alaric clasped my hand and squeezed. "I think somebody might be nervous about our date."

"No, somebody is nervous about a supernatural storm."

Alaric made a dismissive sound. "If this was a supernatural storm, I would've heard from Olis. Trust me, it's fine." He wrapped an arm around me, prompting a stream of fire from George. The vampire cut a glance at the phoenix.

"Knock it off, Sir George, or I'll have your knighthood revoked."

The phoenix seemed agitated. Maybe he was taking the impending move harder than I realized.

We continued along the sidewalk for another block, but I couldn't shake the unease brought on by the unusual sky. "Are we really walking the whole way?"

He shot me a quizzical look. "Since when do you object to walking?"

I pointed to the angry clouds above our heads. "Since a supernatural storm threatened to dump acid rain on us."

Rolling his eyes, the vampire removed his suit jacket and covered my shoulders with it. "If it starts to rain, draw this over your head."

I snuggled under the jacket and continued walking. If I were the sentimental type, I'd make sure to 'forget' to return the jacket to him at the end of the evening. The rational part of me knew it was a bad idea. I had to travel light and that included cramming as many weapons as I could fit into my backpack and suitcase. A lone witch couldn't be too careful.

We entered the theater without incident. No one frisked me or detected my lone weapon. Even better, no one seemed to recognize the king. If they did, they respectfully disguised their excitement.

As we sat, Alaric handed me the program. "Which one is your ex?" I asked, succumbing to my curiosity.

"Minerva has that distinct pleasure."

"Pleasure, yes. Distinct, not so much." I glanced at the photo of the beaming blonde. Go figure. I always knew the king had a type. Like most of his conquests, I was a blonde, but my frame was more toned and athletic, unlike Minerva and her ballasts.

"Too bad Minerva wasn't aboard the Titanic," I whispered. "Those breasts could've saved lives."

"What makes you think she wasn't?"

I scoffed. Minerva wasn't *that* old. If she were, she'd show off the streaks of white that indicated a long-lived vampire. In fact, white hair was worn with pride by most species. Wrinkles and strands of white or grey told the world at a glance that you were a force to be reckoned with. Approach with caution. I aspired to crow's feet and a snowy white head.

The show started with an up-tempo musical number that involved colorful twirling umbrellas and a fountain.

"Are you sure this is *Romeo and Juliet*?" I whispered.

"It's an updated version."

Fragments of plaster dusted my sleeve. Instinctively I tipped my head back. "Does the ceiling look dented to you?"

The woman behind us shushed me.

"Rude," I grumbled. I tried to focus on the actors, but I kept confusing two of the men. The vampires portraying Tybalt and Romeo were physically similar and I wasn't invested enough in their performances to keep them straight.

Alaric leaned over and whispered, "Minerva's good, right?"

"Sure." So far all she had to do was look pretty. Not much of a stretch.

A creaking noise drew my attention back to the ceiling, which was now sagging under the weight of...something. I shifted uncomfortably as a feeling of intense dread washed over me. Larger pieces of plaster plummeted to the floor. A shredding sound followed as the ceiling gave way.

Screams pierced the air as a dark figure dropped from

above. With its gaping maw and hefty body covered in coarse hair, it looked like a cross between a werewolf and a rabid bear. The monster landed center stage, and the actors scrambled to escape. The creature searched the audience as though getting its bearings and then unleashed a roar that shook our seats.

I jumped to my feet and hiked up my dress to reveal the garter. The woman beside me released a gasp of dismay.

"You have pearls right there," I said, motioning to her neck. "Now might be a good time to clutch them."

I whipped the dagger from its hiding spot and launched myself across my neighbors' legs to reach the aisle.

The monster leaped over the orchestra pit and landed at the start of the center aisle only a foot away from me. Its eyes burned with blue fire. The monster was surprisingly fast given its size. It opened its enormous jaws and roared again like a beast staking its turf.

"Sorry, friend. This seat's taken." I sized up my opponent. He was bigger than me, sure, but weren't they always?

The monster swiped an oversized paw at my face. I recoiled and dodged the blow. The sharp claws could do serious damage and I wasn't dressed for combat.

"Not the dress," I warned. "It was a gift."

I lunged forward and thrust the dagger through the thick hide of its chest. I withdrew the dagger and noticed the blade was clean. Did I manage to miss a vessel?

The monster reared up, preparing to strike.

Alaric appeared by my side, wielding a flagpole. I glanced at the gaping hole in the wall next to the stage.

"Is it wrong that I'm mildly turned on right now?" I asked.

"Only mildly?" He used the pole to poke at the monster and keep it at bay.

The hellbeast dove to the left and scampered over the seats. The remaining audience members scattered like marbles. Dagger in hand, I charged after it. I would've preferred something with a longer blade, but ten inches was better than nothing.

If only Liam were here to make an inappropriate joke.

The creature sniffed the air. Its head swiveled left to right as though in search of something.

The actors watched from the shadows of the stage. I noticed Tybalt—or Romeo—wielding a red umbrella as a defensive weapon. My gaze turned to a fanged Alaric with his sleeves pushed up to reveal powerful forearms and a deadly expression. Proof positive that not all vampires were created equal.

I tried to form a connection with the creature, but it was like trying to grab air. I quickly abandoned the effort. I couldn't risk the beast escaping the theater. The chaos would spill over to the streets.

I jumped on the nearest chair and hurdled across the rows toward the beast. Sensing my approach, it craned its neck to glower at me before releasing a ferocious growl that caused the chairs to vibrate. The subtle movement was enough to throw me off balance. My foot slipped as I ran, and I crashed into the seats.

Alaric zipped past me holding the empty flagpole. He raised the pole over his shoulder and flung it like a spear. Unfortunately, without a point at the end, there was no point. The pole bounced off the creature's thick hide and dropped to the floor, rolling to rest against the seats.

I ran down the aisle and lunged at the beast's back. I was vaguely aware of the hem of my dress as it rode up past my underpants. There'd be plenty of time for humiliation later.

Gripping the handle of the dagger, I raised it high in the air and drove it into the creature's neck. The strike was powerful enough to knock the monster on its side. I pulled out the blade and inspected the metal. Still no blood. How did the creature not have any blood? Blood was my access point to victory.

When the monster turned its menacing eyes to me, I seized the opportunity to strike again. I thrust the blade into its eye and *pushed* as far as it would go. The monster's head drooped to the floor.

I turned to Alaric. "I bet you're glad I brought a weapon now, aren't you?"

The vampire stared at the monster as it drew its last, shuddering breath. "What is it?"

"No idea."

Apparently, there wasn't going to be time for a thorough examination either. The monster started to smoke and disappeared in a blue haze.

"Where did it go?" Minerva asked, hesitantly returning to center stage.

I stared at the empty spot on the floor. "Okay, that was a new and deeply unsettling experience."

Minerva clutched the neckline of her shirt. "Why do these things always happen to me?" she whined.

I looked around the theater. "To you?" I repeated, incredulous.

Alaric offered a friendly wave. "It's okay, Minerva. The monster is dead now."

She perked up at the sight of her former paramour. "You saved us, Your Majesty. How brave."

I rolled my eyes. "If you intend to rekindle that particular romance, please wait until I'm safely out of House August territory."

"No fear of that," he whispered.

Gods above. That husky voice was destined to haunt my dreams once I was gone.

"Do you think it got through the ward?" I asked.

"What's the alternative?"

I waved a hand. "Someone let this guy loose in the city."

"Summoning spell?"

"Or raised it from birth." Which begged the question—what gave birth to *that*?

Minerva sat on the edge of the stage with her legs dangling. "Where is everybody? What happened to 'the show must go on?'"

"It'll have to go on without us, I'm afraid." Alaric linked his arm with mine. "Care to accompany me to the compound and we can look into this together?"

I hesitated. "Is that smart?"

"I value your input, Britt. If there's a security issue, you might be able to help."

"And why would I want to do that?"

"Because unlike that guy"—he motioned to where the corpse had been—"you are not a monster."

I hated when he was right. I grabbed his suit jacket from the chair and tightened the edges around my shoulders. "No rest for the wicked."

Alaric offered a seductive grin. "That can be arranged."

Chapter Two

Getting to the compound on foot wasn't easy. The wind had picked up and heavy drops of rain pelted the sidewalk. I used Alaric's jacket as a shield to push my way through the sheets of water.

"No amount of dry cleaning is going to save that jacket," Alaric commented as the guards parted and we entered the private entrance to the royal compound.

"I think you have bigger concerns than a jacket."

"That's why we're going to find Olis right now."

At the mention of Olis, my stomach tightened. I wasn't excited to see my former boss again given our last exchange. I didn't believe for one second the prophecy was real, and I certainly didn't believe I had a role to play. The return of the sun was wishful thinking, an idea that gave the oppressed something to rally around and cling to—not that I blamed them. We all needed a reason to get out of bed and live through another day.

"Do you think he'll know what the monster was?" I asked.

"I don't know, but I can't think of a better person to ask."

A small part of me felt guilty for not sharing the wizard's overture with Alaric. Ultimately, I didn't see the point. Wishful thinking wasn't a genuine threat to House August and Olis was good at his job...Well, aside from looking the other way when wizards set off magic bombs in the city. Then again, I was the one who decided to let those particular rebels go after discovering their activities in a defunct Big Apple tour bus. Maybe I had a twisted loyalty to my kind after all.

As I accompanied Alaric through the large, airy hall of the compound, I felt the stares of the guards. Until recently I'd been an indentured servant, lower than any member of staff. Now I walked beside the king himself as an equal. I knew it rankled many of them, especially those who were aware of my former profession. Whenever I noticed a scowl or a glare aimed at me, I longed to tell them that most of the clients that hired me to kill vampires had been vampires themselves. Vampires with cash to spare were more than happy to use witches and wizards to accomplish what they could not.

The long walk to the security wing reminded me of the compound's impressive size. We were in the working wing, which was far less glamorous than the rooms where the queen regent entertained. Alaric's mother was more interested in fashion and design than administrative matters and it showed. This side of the compound was sterile and joyless, a reminder of King Maxwell's legacy. Alaric's father had been more feared than beloved, even by his own son.

We finally arrived at one of the smaller, windowless rooms in the compound, designed to be private and informal. There was no chance of eavesdropping guards or visitors in here.

Olis stood at the foot of the table. His clothing appeared slightly disheveled as though he'd dressed in a hurry. I wondered if the security breach had interrupted one of his extracurricular activities.

"Good, you're already here," Alaric said.

The wizard bowed slightly. "I heard about the incident at the theater, Your Majesty. I have a security team sweeping the area as we speak."

I examined him closely. Was it possible Olis had heard about it so quickly because his group was involved?

I put the brakes on my train of thought. Not my circus. Not my magical monkeys. The city's problems weren't mine anymore. Besides, Alaric was a capable king. He could handle Trinity Group's diversionary tactics without me—if that's what this was.

"I'm not sure they'll find anything," Alaric said. "The monster disappeared."

Olis pivoted to me. "I was told you slayed the beast."

"I did. At least I think I did. But the body went poof."

The wizard frowned. "I don't suppose you have any insight on the creature."

I shrugged. "I think he lashed out because his mother rejected him, and his father wasn't in the picture."

Olis maintained a neutral expression. As usual, he didn't seem to find my answer amusing. "Were you able to identify the species?"

"Ugly monster. That's a species, right?"

Olis ignored me, hands down his most impressive skill. "Please provide a detailed account of the incident, including a description and how you killed the creature." He slid a paper and pen across the table to me.

"It looked like a cross between a wolf and a bear," Alaric said, shaking droplets of water from his hair.

"You should know we're also monitoring the storm, Your Majesty."

"It's supernatural, right?" I interrupted. "Please tell His Majesty the storm isn't normal."

Olis directed his response to the king. "We're trying to determine whether the storm is connected to the appearance of the monster."

Alaric removed a neatly folded handkerchief from his pocket and wiped the water from his face. "Britt thinks the storm is supernatural."

"At this point it's anybody's guess," Olis replied. "I'm more concerned that the creature knew how to find you."

Alaric's face flickered with surprise. "Me? It seemed to be on the hunt for someone, but I'm not sure I was the target."

I agreed that it didn't seem to register the king's presence. "If someone sent that thing to attack Alaric, they did a poor job of programming it."

Fists pounded on the closed door.

"Enter," Alaric called.

The door swung open and a set of vampires burst through the doorway, soaking wet. I recognized Dudley and Wayne from one of the patrol units.

"Your Majesty, there's a security issue in Sector Four," Dudley said.

Alaric nodded. "We know about the monster, thank you."

Dudley and Wayne exchanged glances. "We don't know anything about a monster, Your Majesty," Wayne said.

"Then what kind of issue?" Olis prompted.

"Part of the ward's down," Dudley said. "We think it's the storm."

"Nonsense," Alaric scoffed. "The ward doesn't run on electricity. It would take a..." His gaze shifted to me.

I tried not to look too smug. "You can say it."

"Supernatural storm," Alaric offered.

"That answers our question as to how the monster got in," I commented.

Olis seemed to snap to attention. "I'll assemble a team immediately."

"Have Calinda do it," Alaric ordered. "Your hands are full at the moment."

Calinda was a witch in charge of the Ward Division. She and her team reported directly to Olis. She and I knew each other only in the vaguest sense, mostly because we both worked in House security. The fact that she was a paid employee and I'd been an indentured servant meant that we didn't really mix. Another day, another pecking order.

"With all due respect, I can handle it, Your Majesty," Olis insisted.

"Very well. That'll be all for now. Go back to your quarters and dry off." Alaric waited for the two vampires to leave before continuing the conversation. "What's your plan, Olis?"

"Seal the breach before it's discovered by more intruders," the wizard said. "The last thing we need is a horde of dragons finding an entry point." He looked at me. "Your little friend excepted."

"Turns out my little friend isn't a dragon after all." Olis was the one who'd identified George as a pygmy dragon. "He's a phoenix."

Olis looked genuinely shocked. "A phoenix? How remarkable."

"I'd like a report on the monster as soon as possible," Alaric said. "If it's connected to the storm, there might be more of them."

"The only ones powerful enough to create a storm that breaks through wards and parachutes in monsters would be another House," I said.

"I'm still not convinced it had anything to do with me," Alaric countered. "No one knew I was there. Unless I was being tracked, my money's on a coincidence."

"If not you, then what could the monster possibly have wanted in a theater?" Olis mused.

"A riveting performance, just like everybody else," I said.

"I wonder if it might've fallen through the roof by accident," Alaric said. "Fell through the ward and straight through to the theater."

"Fell from where? A cloud?" I asked.

"I don't know of any monsters that travel by cloud, Your Majesty," Olis added.

"And it didn't have wings," I said. "It also didn't have blood."

The wizard balked. "No blood? Are you certain?"

I pursed my lips. "Kind of my specialty."

"A breach in the ward and the appearance of a creature not one of us can identify," Alaric said soberly. "I don't like it."

Olis tapped his phone. "I believe the storm is interfering with communications as well, Your Majesty. I've been trying to send a message to Calinda, but it won't go through."

Phones were unreliable at the best of times. A supernatural storm wouldn't help matters.

Alaric plucked the phone from the wizard's hand. "Let

me see if I can have someone in tech take a look at this. I'll be right back."

The vampire exited the room, leaving me alone with Olis.

"Aren't you worried about the king walking off with your phone?" I asked.

"Not in the least. After all, the phone technically belongs to him."

In other words, his personal communications took place via a secret phone. I should've guessed.

I decided to cut to the chase. "Is this monster one of your group's diversionary tactics?"

The wizard recoiled slightly. "Do you seriously think I'd damage a ward in the middle of midtown and put thousands of lives at risk?"

"Your friends set off a magic bomb in the subway. Why would this be a bridge too far?"

He raised an eyebrow. "And here I thought you were leaving New York. Need I remind you that your unwillingness to join the cause has made you a target? The sooner you go, the safer you'll be."

"I highly doubt it. If I'm as important as you claim, nobody would dare harm me."

"They might not harm you directly. That doesn't mean they won't find other ways to hurt you."

"Like sending a bloodless monster after the king, knowing I was with him and wouldn't be able to protect him using my magic?"

The wizard and I stared at each other for a beat too long.

"On my honor, I had nothing to do with it," he insisted. "I will continue to uphold my duties to this House."

"Minotaur shit. You broke that oath when you turned a blind eye to your criminal friends."

"As did you." His face relaxed. "I have no grievance with His Majesty specifically. In fact, I've grown rather fond of him. I only wish to return the world to its natural state."

"Then how do you explain your wizard friends? Their bombs are supposed to do what—be so potent they shake the sun out of hiding?"

"They're a minor distraction, nothing more."

"They're lucky they haven't managed to kill anyone."

"For a marginalized individual, you seem awfully fond of the current world order. You might want to reevaluate your priorities."

I bristled. "I'm free now, remember?"

"It doesn't make you one of them and it never will. You know this already, though, don't you? It's the reason you've decided to leave, despite your feelings for His Majesty." His mouth clamped shut when Alaric reentered the room.

The king returned the wizard's phone. "Should work better now. You were missing an update."

"Thank you, Your Majesty. You're most kind."

"Nothing kind about it. We have an emergency and I need you to be able to communicate with your team. Now, what have I missed?"

"Only an exchange of theories, Your Majesty," Olis said quickly. "Isn't that right, Britt?"

I wasn't sure what to think, so I decided to play along. If Olis was involved, my best bet was to let him think I believed him. "I was just about to give Olis a more detailed description of the creature." I proceeded to write an honest account of the encounter. There was no point in holding back—the wizard either already knew because he'd orchestrated it, or he wasn't involved and needed the information to perform his duties.

Olis took the paper from me once I finished. "I'll let you know the moment I learn anything, Your Majesty."

"If you don't find anything, then check with other Houses. Use every resource at your disposal."

"Are you certain you want to confer with other Houses, Your Majesty?" Olis asked. "What if one of them is behind the attack?"

Alaric dragged a hand through his thick waves. "I really don't think...Ah, fine. Start with House Nilsson." The second largest House in North America had been the primary adversary of House August until the death of King Maxwell brought the two Houses together. Alaric and I had even fought alongside royal siblings, Genevieve and Michael.

"Right away, Your Majesty." Olis hurried from the room, averting his gaze as he passed me.

I touched Alaric's arm. "You seem more on edge now than you did in the theater."

"I've had time to process."

"Security will patch the hole in the ward," I assured him. "No more unexpected drop-ins. And hopefully the storm will pass quickly."

"I don't think you should leave the city until this has been resolved," Alaric said. "It's too dangerous."

"For me or for you?"

He reached for my hand. "Stay here tonight. It's the safest place you can be."

"You'll be preoccupied. You don't need me here to distract you."

His thumb stroked the inside of my wrist. "On the contrary. I can't think of a more welcome distraction."

I withdrew my hand. "I'll be fine. It's only a short walk to the apartment and George will be worried if I don't come home."

"In that case, I'll escort you."

I laughed. "Alaric, I think we both know I'm perfectly capable of taking care of myself." After the death of Alaric's father, I was the one who'd safely escorted the would-be king from his Palm Beach estate to New York City. Not the easiest journey I'd ever undertaken, but we lived to tell the tale.

"I'll feel better knowing you're safe," he said.

"You're going to have to get used to uncertainty when it comes to me," I advised. "Once I leave the city, I don't know how frequently we'll be in touch."

His mouth tightened. "Way to kick me when I'm down."

I blew out a breath. "I'm sorry. I'm also sorry our date didn't go as planned." Although I couldn't pretend to be surprised. Nothing between us had ever gone as planned. Another reason it was best to go our separate ways.

"Don't leave tomorrow without saying goodbye," he said. "That's a royal command."

"I won't." His powerful arms were too much to resist and I folded into them. "Good night, Your Majesty."

Two guards escorted me through the compound to the private exit. In my best dress, I easily blended in with the vampires out and about for the evening. There was an unspoken hierarchy in the city, with the epicenter being House August. The closer you lived and worked to the compound, the more affluent you were. Although there were other species occupying the same neighborhood, they generally had some kind of special status like Olis and Liam. The farther away you were from the compound, the number of shifters, magic users, and humans increased—unless you went underground. Over the past few decades humans had gathered there en masse to escape the notice of vampires.

As I crossed the street, I was relieved to see the sky had returned to its usual charcoal palette. Maybe that meant the ward had been successfully sealed. Despite the return to normalcy, I felt the same sense of unease I'd experienced earlier and traced it to my conversation with Olis. I'd believed the Trinity Group wasn't a real threat to Alaric, that their dream of bringing back the sun was pie in the sky. But what if I was wrong? What if they were growing bolder in their efforts? Olis's denial had seemed sincere...

I decided to trust, but verify.

Out of the corner of my eye, I spotted a silhouette huddled against a wall in a dark alley. The blanket and cardboard box suggested he was homeless. I ground to a halt when I noticed two vampires approaching him. Like most humans, homeless people tended to stay below ground to avoid becoming food for opportunistic predators. House August had clamped down on the behavior in recent years, but it remained a problem as long as human blood was the main source of sustenance. I'd heard rumors of a trial phase of synthetic blood, as well as the development of a vaccine that made human blood taste abhorrent to vampires. So far, neither effort had gone mainstream.

I joined the two vampires in the alley where they towered over the homeless man.

"Gentlemen, I'm going to need you to step away from the man," I said, adopting an authoritative voice.

"Says who?" the first vampire asked. His square jaw and sinister eyes seemed in sharp contrast to his attire, which included a yellow bowtie and paisley vest.

"King Alaric of House August. Ever hear of him?"

His companion looked me over like he was studying the specials menu at a blood bank. "You're the concubine."

My hands clenched into fists. "I beg your pardon."

"The harlot," he added, as though I'd misunderstood the word 'concubine.'

I folded my arms and offered him my thousand-yard stare. "The name is Death Bringer."

The second vampire snorted. "And who do you bring death to?"

I forged a connection with his blood and tugged. "First, it's 'to whom do I bring death?'"

The vampire's eyes widened as he felt the odd sensation of a third party seizing control of his blood.

Gently I pressed the brake and slowed his blood flow. "Second, I think with a little due diligence, you'll find I mainly bring death to vampires." I flashed a friendly smile and *pushed* the blood.

The vampire released a strangled cry and clutched his chest. The square-jawed vampire gaped at his companion and then at me. As he advanced toward me, my magic reached for his blood, too. It took me a moment to be sure that I'd made contact with the second vampire and not latched onto more of his companion's blood. My experience with handling two targets at once was relatively new, as I'd only recently discovered the ability in the Wasteland.

Maintaining my hold on them, I made eye contact with the would-be victim. "Go," I ordered.

The man picked up his threadbare blanket and ran. I waited until the darkness swallowed him to release my hold on the vampires. Panting, they glowered at me.

"Remember this moment the next time you want to refer to a woman as a concubine or a harlot." There was a small risk they'd report me for the unauthorized use of magic, but it was more likely they wouldn't want to repeat their accusation to the king.

"You're a witch. What do you care what happens to a walking snack pack?" the square-jawed vampire asked.

"I care," was all I said. Just because I was no longer an indentured servant on the security team didn't mean I stopped caring about the city's more vulnerable residents. Without magic, that homeless man could've been me.

I continued to my apartment—not to sleep as Alaric believed, but to change. If I was going to launch an independent investigation of the mystery monster, I needed to dress the part.

Chapter Three

The rain had tapered off by the time I sat on the windowsill of my apartment, watching the skyline for any sign of unusual activity. I'd changed into comfortable clothes and work boots. My suitcase remained half empty and the map was still folded. My future could wait another few hours. Right now, I had other priorities.

George sat beside me. I'd told him about the eventful evening and that I intended to do a little recon before I left. I had to confirm that Olis and his compatriots weren't behind the theater attack. I owed that much to Alaric.

A few blocks away, a cluster of butterflies headed north of the compound, away from the theater. It wasn't a regular patrol either. Their schedule was like clockwork and this wasn't it. Maybe the storm had caused damage uptown that required attention.

"Where do you think those butterflies are headed?"

George cocked his head as if to say, 'beats me.'

I swung my feet inside. "Can you follow them? I'll catch up."

George spread his wings and took off.

I strapped on two daggers and raced to the ground floor. I'd have to follow the phoenix from street level, which wasn't ideal. It would be hard to see George amidst the blinding city lights. While I appreciated House August's efforts to maintain the illusion of daylight, it currently interfered with my goal of tracking the diminutive phoenix.

George flew straight up Eighth Avenue. The earlier crowds had thinned, which made it easier to track the phoenix. I only lost sight of him once. When I glimpsed him on a streetlight, I was about to ask why he stopped until I realized our location—Central Park. There was no sign of the butterfly patrol.

I peered up at George. "Where'd they go?"

He blew a puff of smoke in the direction of the park.

"No." I gave an adamant shake of my head. "There's no way they'd go in there." Not voluntarily at least.

Once upon a time Central Park had been a thriving space in the middle of the city for residents to enjoy. Those days were long over. In an Eternal Night world, the park had grown into over eight hundred acres of mangled swamp. It was often described as a sprawling spider that trapped and devoured whatever became ensnared in its wide web. House August didn't bother to send patrols past the four streets that surrounded the park. It was considered too high a cost for too little benefit. In Olis's opinion, anybody that strayed too close to Central Park deserved their fate, which made the presence of a butterfly patrol in the vicinity even more puzzling.

I contemplated the park from the southwest corner of Fifty-Ninth and Eighth. I refused to leave Alaric in a dangerous situation that I could've prevented. "What do you say, George? One last hurrah before we leave the city?"

George squawked his approval.

There were no official entrances to the park anymore. If you wanted in, you had to cut through the muck. Best to wear thigh-high rubber boots if you were lucky enough to own a pair.

I wasn't that lucky.

I glanced down at my favorite footwear. "RIP boots."

I ventured forward and my left boot immediately sank into a sticky mud pit. Wonderful.

"Any sign of the patrol?" I asked.

George swooped ahead, returning a moment later with a sagging head. Maybe he was mistaken and the patrol turned left or continued straight past the park.

A roar emanated from the heart of the swamp that shook the ground beneath my feet. Jackpot.

I started in the direction of the sound. From this distance, I couldn't decide whether it was the same roar as the bloodless beast in the theater. If it was, at least I knew how to kill it.

George flapped his wings excitedly and I followed his gaze skyward where the same cluster of butterflies flew at a rapid pace in the direction of the compound. Whatever they'd witnessed in the park, they were in a hurry to report it. It also meant the roaring creature had been left untouched. By the time a security team returned, the monster could be terrorizing Lincoln Center. I couldn't risk it.

George blew a swath of fire at the swampy growth, effectively clearing a path for me.

I tipped an imaginary hat. "Thank you kindly, Sir George."

We forged ahead and I suddenly wished I had more than two daggers on me. I wasn't planning on a recon mission through the abyss known as Central Park, but here we were. It wouldn't be the first time I'd dived headfirst into trouble.

I kicked aside dark, slimy vines and listened for any further noise from the monster. Pre-Eternal Night, there'd been a zoo here. According to reports, the animals broke free after the Great Eruption and roamed the city. Some terrorized the residents; others crossed the border and kept running. There were rumors that descendants of the original zoo animals still inhabited the city, but I'd never seen any evidence of it.

The plants that thrived in the park were different from the ones sustained by witches and wizards. These plants were infused with magic of a different sort, more wild and mystical. Ancient magic that escaped from the earth's core like the monsters themselves.

The air felt thick here and a foul odor emanated from the damp ground. The sudden rainfall must've stirred up the marsh.

The crack of vines stopped me in my tracks. George hovered above me, awaiting my signal. I surveyed the darkness, careful not to move and give away my location.

A pair of red eyes blazed through the murk, looking off to the right. Based on their height, I'd judge the monster to be at least six feet. Terrific. A dagger was best at close range. Although my aim was excellent, I didn't want to hurl it across the swamp and lose it in the shadows.

"What big eyes you have, Grandma," I whispered. I crept forward and tried to stick to the soft mud so I could launch a sneak attack. Of course, there was every chance this guy could smell me. I passed multiple kebab vendors on the way here and those scents stick to your skin like a good lotion.

George wisely kept to the shadows above me. He'd be

my firepower should the need arise, and there was every chance it would.

A guttural sound stopped me in my tracks and the back of my neck pricked. It wasn't the sound of a wolf or a bear. It was deeper and far more menacing.

Oh, joy.

I withdrew a dagger and waited.

A forked tongue flicked through a set of sharp fangs. The creature seemed to be tasting the air.

Not tasting—smelling.

The monster's red eyes were apparently for show because they couldn't see me. It was resorting to its sense of smell. I jumped to the left as its tail came careening toward me. It crashed into a mass of twisted vines and that's when I saw the other head perched on the end of the tail.

Okay, I did not have two-headed serpent on my monster bingo card. What kind of serpent made a guttural sound?

"You should hiss," I told the monster, as though my complaint mattered.

The serpent growled in response.

Four sets of red eyes now fixated on me. At least they were easy to see in the gloaming. The head to my left shot toward me and I darted back a few steps, still clutching the dagger. There was no point in stabbing an eye when there were three more to find me, plus two forked tongues. I wasn't even sure what this growling two-headed serpent could do. I debated whether this was preferable to the monster in the theater.

That depended on how fast I could kill it.

The serpent was faster than I anticipated and immediately had me on the defensive. I was too busy dodging heads on either end to forge a connection with its blood. One head attacked while the other waited its turn. At a certain point I realized they had a strategy. Keep me playing defense and wear me down.

Good luck with that.

The second head reared up, preparing to strike again. This time I changed the game. With a dagger in each hand, I jumped between the heads and landed on the serpent's back. Both heads came toward me at once. I ducked and their faces crashed together. I used the moment to my advantage and sliced downward with both hands, carving their necks with parallel lines. Black liquid oozed from their matching wounds, followed by a putrid odor. It wasn't a full beheading, but it was good enough.

I jumped to the ground and wiped the blades on an obliging vine as the serpent drew a final, shuddering breath.

"Fangs for the memories." I hesitated. "Too soon?"

I spun around at the sound of crunching vines. Not another one. The park seemed as rife as the Monster Maze in the Wasteland. Was there a wizard living in the abandoned zoo and commanding them? If that was the case, I'd need reinforcements.

My thumb stroked the handle of my dagger. The shadow moved. I counted one man-sized head.

"Who's there?" I demanded.

A silhouette cut through the shadows, revealing a red scar that burned bright in the darkness. I recognized that topographical face anywhere.

"I know you," I said. He was one of the wizards I'd encountered in the Big Apple tour bus. I was beginning to worry my suspicions about Olis were valid. The realization wasn't satisfying.

"Help me," the wizard croaked. He pitched forward and I caught him before he faceplanted in the mud.

"What are you doing here?"

He shook his head, either unwilling or unable to talk.

"Are you alone or with your friends?"

"Help them," he said in a hoarse voice.

"Why are you here? Did you have something to do with the Gemini snake?"

His gaze dropped to the ground.

"The more you tell me, the better chance I have of helping your friends."

"Messing with the ward."

"*A* ward or *the* ward?" I didn't know why I bothered to ask. I already knew the answer.

He pointed above our heads to indicate the city ward. "Attacked before we could finish."

I cursed under my breath. "By any chance were you messing with the ward in the theater district, too?"

Confusion marred his already-blemished features.

"Did you summon the monster?" I prodded.

The wizard shook his head. "Will you help them?"

"What kind of magic do they have?"

His face contorted. "What does it matter?"

"I'm the one asking the questions now."

He squeezed his eyes closed. "Spells."

"What kind of spells?" For someone who wanted my help, he was being deliberately vague.

He didn't respond.

I tapped my wrist. "Tick tock, friend. I can drag you out of here right now and leave your friends to their fate, but I expect that wouldn't make you very popular with your rebel buddies."

He licked his lips and his gaze darted to the left, as though he could picture his companions just out of reach. "Potions."

I highly doubted the potions they carried to break the ward would help them in a monster fight.

"Show me the way."

The wizard remained rooted to the ground. He seemed conflicted about returning from the place he'd just escaped. It wasn't like he could offer simple directions through the park.

"If you want my help, you have to show me."

Reluctantly, he stumbled through the swamp and I followed close behind.

"What made you choose Central Park?" I complained. "This place is already chaos without you guys adding to it."

He stopped at an entrance to a tunnel beneath an old bridge and pointed. He clung to the shadows, clearly unwilling to venture inside.

As I inched forward with my daggers drawn, it occurred to me this could be a trap. If so, it seemed terribly elaborate. There were much easier ways to capture me.

I reached out to feel for blood. One of the wizards must've sensed my presence because he whispered, "Hurry, before it comes back!"

My eyes weren't adjusting to the pitch dark. I considered using George as a torch but didn't want to risk drawing attention to us with a bright flame.

"Are you tied up?" I asked the shadows.

"Vines."

The serpent I'd encountered had two heads but no opposable thumbs or pincers. "What kind of monster?"

"Some kind of giant ant monster. Hurry!"

I cut through the first thick vine I reached. The two wizards guided me through the rest. We escaped the tunnel and raced through the swamp before the monster returned for a midnight snack.

"Any more of you in the park?" I asked, once we reached a safe distance from the bridge. There'd been four of them in the bus but only three now.

The redhead I'd dubbed Clifford shook his head. "Just us this time."

"You've traded magic bombs for breaking wards? Why the change?"

Nobody answered. Shocker.

"Serves you right to be hoisted by your own petards," I said. "Maybe next time you'll think twice. The ward is there for your benefit as well as everybody else's."

"I'd sic monsters on the whole city if it meant toppling the vampire regime," Scarface said.

"You can't paint all vampires with the same brush. Alaric's a good king."

"Does he feed on you?"

I whipped toward Clifford. "Excuse me?"

"Do you two have some kind of symbiotic relationship like a barnacle and a whale?"

My hands rested on my hips. "Which one of us is the whale in that scenario?"

He cringed. "Is there a wrong answer?"

I glared at him. "What do you think?"

"You're going to end up on the wrong side of history, witch," the scarred wizard said. "Join us now before it's too late."

"Join the monster mash? No thanks. I'm on my way out of the city."

They exchanged glances. "For good?" the third wizard asked.

I shrugged. "For now. Got my bags packed and everything." Almost.

"Then what are you doing in the middle of Central Park?" the scarred one asked.

"Saving your sorry ass, apparently." I folded my arms and regarded them. "Does Olis know about this?"

Once again, my question was met with silence.

"You know the price for using magic. If House August finds out, you'll be executed."

Clifford gave me a long look. "You weren't."

"Only because I agreed to servitude. Is that what you want?"

"Dunno. Will I get the same choice?"

"I honestly don't know."

I contemplated my options. I'd already let these wizards go once. For Alaric's sake, I'd be a fool to do it again. On the other hand, I couldn't bring myself to condemn them to death. I'd been in their shoes once and had been given a reprieve.

I tugged my phone from my pocket and hoped the park wasn't too dense for reception.

"Have you learned something?" Olis asked.

"Not sure. Still trying to figure that out." Despite my suspicions, I decided Olis was the right one to contact under the circumstances. I'd leave their fate in the wizard's hands. He'd been aghast at the accusation I'd leveled at him regarding the Sector Four ward. Let's see how he handled a threat to the ward by his own people.

I wasn't surprised when Olis showed up personally to collect the lawbreakers. Although he brought a small team, there wasn't a vampire among them. I bet there would be no report filed with House August either. I couldn't decide whether it was because Olis was skittish like me when it came to condemning magic users or because he was more involved than he claimed.

"These guys sure like to cause chaos," I remarked. "They were trying to punch a hole through the ward and got snagged by an ant monster looking for a picnic."

Olis appeared distracted. "Yes, a hole in the park ward would've been particularly worrisome. This area attracts more monsters than the rest of the city combined."

I shot him a speculative look. "I thought these guys worked for you."

He kept his troubled gaze on the trio. "As did I."

I felt torn. Once again, the wizard's response seemed sincere. "I don't feel right keeping this from Alaric."

This got his attention. "Then I'm sure you realize you'll have the blood of three wizards on your hands."

"I'm not sure that'll be my fault." Then again, I had enough blood on my hands. Did I really want to add to the tally? "What if they're responsible for the hole in Sector Four?" Just because their attempt failed here didn't mean they hadn't succeeded at the theater.

"I'll handle them," Olis said. "This isn't your job anymore, remember?"

I couldn't handle the uncertainty. "Swear to me you had nothing to do with this."

The wizard flinched. "Do you realize how dangerous this would be for everyone in the city?"

"Oh, I realize. I wasn't sure if you cared."

Olis placed a hand on my shoulder and looked me in the eye. "I had nothing to do with this, nor the incident at the theater. I swear to you. Do you think I would've revealed my secret to you if I intended greater harm to the king or the city?"

"It could've been a tactical admission." I missed the days of antagonizing Olis for fun. Life seemed simpler then.

The wizard rubbed his weary eyes. "Perhaps if you

came to a meeting, you would have a better understanding of our cause."

"And then what?"

He shrugged. "And then I'd regain your trust."

Did I need to trust him if I was leaving the city anyway? I did, especially if I planned to leave him as Alaric's right-hand man.

"I'll think about it."

His smile was almost imperceptible. "Does that mean you're not leaving tomorrow?"

Now it was my turn to avoid an answer.

Once the wizards left, I staggered out of the park, feeling emotionally and physically drained. I felt droplets on my back as blood dripped from the ends of my hair. I wasn't even sure where it came from. I'd be grossed out later. Right now I needed to get home before I collapsed. Every muscle was on fire. George seemed as beat as I was. The phoenix didn't have his usual spring in his wing flap.

According to Liam, there were horse-drawn carriages in and around the park in the pre-Eternal Night world. I'd pay good money for one of those right now, as long as the horses weren't mistreated, of course. I'd fall asleep to the rhythmic sound of hooves clip-clopping on the street.

George stayed in protective mode, hovering only a foot above my head. A bell rang as a rickshaw pulled alongside me.

I gave the driver a meek look. "No money," I said.

He motioned me forward.

"I can't. I'll get blood and goo all over your ride."

He turned and lifted an object from beside him. A folded blanket. He draped the blanket across the backseat and gestured to me again.

Grateful, I gave him the address and climbed into the

back where I promptly curled into a ball on the blanket. Never underestimate the kindness of strangers.

I took a catnap between the park and my apartment building. I only knew I'd arrived because the driver gently shook me awake.

"Thank you so much," I said. "Your kindness will not be forgotten."

He smiled, showing a couple broken teeth. I realized with a start they'd once been fangs. The driver was a vampire. Between the silence and the teeth, there was a story there—most likely a depressing one.

"Stay safe," I said for lack of a better parting remark.

I dragged myself into the building and up the stairwell. I barely managed to unlock the door. All I wanted to do was wash away the grime and gore and fall into a deep sleep devoid of nightmares.

The sound of running water startled me. "Hello?"

"Finally. I thought you were coming straight home from the compound." Alaric emerged from the bathroom. Dressed in a crisp, white shirt and tight black trousers, the vampire looked like a sexy slice of heaven. His smile faded as his gaze passed over me. "What happened?"

My knees buckled. "I'm okay," I squeaked.

Strong arms scooped me off the floor and carried me across the room to the bathroom. Bubbles billowed over the edge of the tub as a candle burned at each end. He set me down but continued to keep a supportive arm around me.

"Why are you here running a bath?" I asked. Even to my own ears, my voice sounded dreamy.

"I wanted to make up for the theater. Our last night together is supposed to be romantic and memorable. It shouldn't involve a mystery monster and a broken ward."

I managed a smile. "Well, you got the memorable part down pat."

He sniffed my neck. "I think I might be psychic because you need a bath more than anything in the world right now."

I didn't disagree.

"Tell me what happened. More monsters?"

How to explain without revealing too much? "I took care of it."

"You always do. Now let me take care of you." His gaze met mine and stayed there.

My desire for the vampire was stronger than my fatigue. "I can't manage these buttons."

His gaze lowered to observe my shirt. "You're not wearing any buttons."

"Then I guess that makes your job easier."

He helped me perch on to the edge of the bath and started by removing my boots. "Holy hellfire. Where were you? These boots are filthy."

"Trust me. If you want to preserve the mood, you don't want to know."

"I am wholly in favor of preserving the mood." He stripped off my clothes with slow, deliberate movements and made a show of folding each item carefully in a pile on the counter next to the sink.

"No need to fold. I'll probably burn them tomorrow."

He frowned when he removed my vest, followed quickly by my shirt. "No bra?"

"You sound disappointed. I'd think this is a shortcut."

He shrugged. "I'm a sucker for a nice, lacy bra."

"You're a sucker, period. And I was fighting monsters, Your Majesty. Pardon me for not dressing up for the occasion."

"You're not supposed to be fighting monsters. You don't work for me anymore, remember?" He eased me into the water and I groaned as the water warmed my skin. The ache in my muscles dissipated as I relaxed and lowered myself amidst the bubbles.

Alaric started to undress.

"What do you think you're doing?" I asked.

"I was planning to join you."

"Sorry, Your Majesty. I think I need to recuperate first."

He lingered by the tub. "And how long do you anticipate this recovery process will take? Need I remind you there's a ticking clock thanks to your hasty exit plan."

"Here's the deal. You can get in if we can talk about what happened. I can't tell you if my mouth is otherwise engaged."

Alaric arched an eyebrow. "And what if my mouth is otherwise engaged?"

"At ease, soldier."

He smirked. "You would refuse His Majesty?"

I sank deeper into the water. "All day every day."

He flicked a knot of bubbles at my face. "To the gallows with you!"

"I fought a two-headed serpent in Central Park." I took the opportunity to dip below the surface and wash the filth from my hair. Of course, now I was simply sitting in the filth which didn't seem much better.

"From another hole in the ward?" Alaric asked when I surfaced. "Two holes in one night?"

"I'm sure that isn't a first for you," I quipped. "But no. I think this monster was already living there." It took all my resolve not to tell him the rest of the story. I needed a distraction. "Get in. You can touch my legs while I tell you more about the monster."

"Well, when you make it so enticing." He removed his clothing and climbed into the tub.

I tried not to ogle his body, but it was like asking a drunkard to walk a straight line. "You're too close. I can't focus." Admittedly, that was kind of the plan.

His mouth twisted in a grin. "I'm not really sure how to fix that. Either you want me in the tub or you don't."

I most definitely did.

"I'll help you stay on track. Was the monster the same as the one from the theater?"

"No." Resting my calf against his powerful thigh, I described the serpent right down to its red eyes.

"Well, you know what they say," Alaric mused. "Two heads are better than one."

"Seriously. Dad jokes at a time like this?"

"There's always time for a dad joke."

"Did your father ever tell jokes?" I couldn't picture the former king dropping humor bombs on the regular.

"I think you know the answer to that question."

"Do you have any idea what the monster is?"

"No, but I'll pass the information..."

"Along to Olis." I sighed. "Yes, I know."

His brow furrowed. "You'd like me to do something else?"

I hesitated. "Maybe not rely so much on Olis."

Alaric smiled. "He's my Director of Security, Britt. If I can't rely on him, then I need to hire someone else."

Fair point.

"What about your research team? Can we also give them the description? Olis must be so busy right now."

"Good idea."

A sense of relief washed over me. I hated feeling so conflicted. Olis was my former boss and annoyed me to no end—or more accurately I annoyed him—but he was still a living, breathing wizard who could've treated an indentured servant like me with far less respect and dignity, except for the occasional boot polish as punishment for insubordination. As genuine as the wizard's denials seemed, however, I couldn't shake my discomfort.

I chose to focus on what I could control—this moment with Alaric. "You, me, bubbles, candlelight, and monster chat. You wanted a romantic evening together and here it is."

His expression darkened. "I could do without the threats to your life."

"It's Central Park. I expect there to be strange creatures lurking in there."

He cocked his head. "How did you end up there in the first place?"

I didn't have a good answer for that. "Habit. I'm still accustomed to dealing with threats to your security."

His grin broadened. "*My* security? That's sweet."

I shifted in the tub. "You seem awfully relaxed for a king under siege."

He laughed. "I'm hardly under siege. For now, I'll let Olis handle the details."

And there it was again. "Olis must be so overwhelmed. Maybe have Calinda..."

Alaric cut me off. "We're naked in the bath. Can we perhaps talk about Olis and Calinda at a more appropriate time? The tub is beginning to feel crowded."

"Since when do you object to a crowded tub?"

He shook his head. "You know those days are over, Britt. If you stay, I'll prove it to you."

I wished I didn't believe him. It would make everything so much easier.

Beneath the water, his fingers found my leg and began to knead my calf muscles. A soft moan escaped my lips.

"You like that, do you?" A sly grin emerged. "There's more where that came from. A lot more."

Unable to resist the overture, I slipped further down the side of the bath to give him access to the rest of my body. The surface of the water lapped against my cheeks.

He arched an eyebrow. "Willing to drown? My skills must be more impressive than I realize."

I blew bubbles across the surface of the water.

"We can drain it a little," he offered.

"Nope. I want to have my cake and eat it, too."

His grin turned devilish. "There is so much I like about that statement."

I turned my head toward the open door and whistled. "George, the water's getting cold. We need a little heat in here."

"Oh, I think we're generating plenty of our own," Alaric replied.

George flew into the room and hovered above the tub. He blew a stream of flames at the water until it bubbled. The warmth soaked into my skin.

I shot Alaric a triumphant look. "Hot tub."

"Much obliged, Sir George," the king said.

George turned and flew out of the bathroom. He liked the vampire better than he once did, but I still wouldn't say they were besties.

"I thought he might roast me," Alaric said.

"He knows what he's doing. Not our first time."

The king smirked. "There are many ways to interpret that statement."

I splashed his face.

"You dare splash the king," he declared with mock indignation. He grabbed my legs and pulled me under.

I burst through the surface, laughing and sputtering water. Bubbles clung to my hair and nose. I climbed over him to sit on his side of the tub. We squeezed together, skin against skin. My heart pounded. There was something about Alaric that turned me inside out. It didn't matter what happened in our past. He wasn't that vampire anymore. He'd grown—matured.

"I hate to leave you," I whispered.

His lips trailed along the curve of my bare shoulder. "Then don't."

I reconsidered my plan. Maybe it was best to stay a bit longer. Between the wizards, the storm, and the strange monster, I felt unsettled. If I left now and something terrible happened, I'd never forgive myself.

"I'll postpone temporarily," I said.

Alaric drew back to look at me. "Only temporarily?"

I splashed his chest. "Take what you can get."

His hand dipped beneath the surface to explore the rest of me. "Oh, believe me. I am."

Chapter Four

Alaric didn't leave my side until morning, when multiple messages forced him back to the compound before he was ready. As I changed clothes, my phone lit up with a call from Olis.

"His Majesty is on his way back to the compound as we speak."

"I'm not calling for the king. I'm calling for you. As long as you're still in the city, I'd like your assistance."

"You know I'm supposed to leave today."

"All packed and ready to go then?"

I cast a guilty glance at my half empty suitcase. "Okay, fine. I postponed."

I could practically hear his snicker. "I'm shocked, I tell you."

"If you want my help, you might want to be nicer."

"Meet me in front of the theater in twenty minutes. I'll explain there."

"Back to the scene of the crime, huh?"

"A little lower than that, I'm afraid."

"The subway? Okay. For underground work, my price is a coffee and a croissant. Extra flaky."

"I'll see what I can do."

I scanned the apartment for George. The phoenix had disappeared at some point during the night, probably to hunt. That made two of us. I strapped on a couple weapons. If I was monster-hunting, I wanted to be better equipped than I was yesterday.

Olis stood on the sidewalk in front of the disused subway entrance closest to the theater and I was delighted to notice a cup of coffee and brown bag in his hand.

"You came through," I said, swiping the offering from his outstretched hand. As I bit into the croissant, a thought occurred to me. "Is this bribery? You think one breakfast will silence me?"

"Do you really think so little of me? This is about the monster you fought here." His gaze slid to the theater. "I believe this incident was unrelated to the one in the park."

"What are the odds of that?"

"An unfortunate coincidence."

"Then why are we here?"

"Because I ran a diagnostic spell to locate anything unusual in this area."

"You're a day late and a dollar short, Olis. The bloodless monster is done and dusted."

"Not the monster itself. You suggested the beast was hunting for something—and I might have found it." His brow creased. "Almost."

"Almost?"

"Whatever it is, it's below ground."

"And you want me to accompany you? Aw, that's so sweet."

"What I want is for you to trust me."

I glanced at the pavement to avoid meeting his gaze. "Your spell picked up activity down there?"

"Not activity necessarily. Something unusual."

"And you think this unusual thing is related to our monster friend in the theater?"

"I can't be certain, of course, but it's worth exploring."

"Why not send a team?"

Olis allowed himself a small smile. "Do I detect a note of uncertainty in your voice? Not to worry, Britt. I have no intention of sequestering you in the tunnels."

"Good, because I don't want to have to kill you."

The wizard and I descended the steps into complete darkness.

"Just like old times, huh? Me and you hitting the tunnels." To be fair, Olis rarely ventured below ground. The wizard rarely did anything that involved grunt work. "Does Alaric know we're here?"

"You might want to remain quiet for this part," he whispered as we reached the bottom. "We have no idea what we might find down here."

I wolfed down my croissant and swallowed the last of the coffee. I'd fight better on a semi-full stomach.

Olis paused to conjure a spell that created light, allowing us to see a few feet ahead.

"Imagine if you could do that spell for the whole world. Sunlight problem solved." I made a show of dusting off my hands.

He turned to observe me but said nothing.

"Lighten up, Olis. Oh wait, you have."

A quiet groan escaped him. "Do you have no regard for your safety?" he asked in a harsh whisper. "Not another word until we find what we're looking for."

"How will we know when we find it?"

He brought a finger to his lips in one sharp motion.

I didn't like following him blindly—or anyone else for that matter—but I submitted.

We crept through the tunnel in silence. Given our location directly beneath a busy section of the city, I was surprised by the quiet atmosphere. There were distant sounds all around us, although nothing that rang any alarm bells.

Olis motioned for me to enter an adjacent tunnel. This one was smaller with walls covered in bright and colorful graffiti. 'Freedom' was written in huge, cloud-like letters.

"Members of your gang?" I asked.

Olis continued walking.

"How can you wear two faces? Don't you see what a dangerous game you're playing? No matter how much the king likes you, he'll do what's necessary..."

Olis stopped abruptly and turned to me. "We all do what's necessary, Britt. You and I wouldn't be down here right now if we didn't."

"Did you let the wizards go again?"

He resumed walking. "I did not. They're in containment, awaiting sentencing. I do not condone the poking of holes in the city ward."

Well, knock me over with a phoenix feather. "Did they claim responsibility for the theater?"

"No, their efforts were limited to the park."

"Their unsuccessful efforts."

"A blessing for us all."

"You're a complex creature, Olis."

"You're one to talk."

As we reached a convergence of tunnels, I heard a strange scratching sound. I pinched the wizard's sleeve.

"Sounds like digging," he whispered.

We peered around the corner into the pitch-dark of the left-side tunnel. The floor of the tunnel had cracked open and a figure descended into the depths below.

No, wait.

Rose.

The figure was *rising* from the depths below.

I tugged the wizard's sleeve. "Are you seeing this?"

"No, I've suddenly lost the power of sight."

I ignored his sarcasm, too intent on the scene unfolding. "What is that thing?"

It looked like a hairless dog, except much bigger and much uglier. Like my opponent in the theater, its eyes glowed like two blue flames.

Olis's face remained impassive. No wonder he was in charge of security. Almost nothing rattled him.

I focused on the creature and tried to form a connection with its blood. If I could slow the blood flow and subdue the creature, it would give us time to capture it and figure out what it was. This uptick in unrecognizable species was unsettling, to say the least.

The monster seemed to sense our presence—or maybe it sensed me poking and prodding it—because it turned its head in our direction.

I pulled Olis around the corner before the creature spotted us.

"I'm going to need you to put on your wizard hat," I said.

"Why? Can't you control it?"

"I'm trying, but it doesn't seem to have any blood."

"Another one? How extraordinary." Olis murmured an incantation under his breath. He was a wily wizard, always managing to perform his spells in a way that didn't reveal their details. Arguably my magic also revealed nothing to observers, but that was the nature of blood magic. Spells were only hidden if the conjurer desired them to be, which Olis most definitely did.

The creature sniffed the air and angled its head toward us.

Uh oh.

The beast charged. Given its bulky size, it moved faster than expected. Razor-like claws swiped at the wizard's face. Blood gushed from the wound.

I grabbed its muzzle with my free hand and thrust the blade of a dagger into the side of its neck. A stupid move on my part. No blood meant no carotid artery.

The hairless dog-monster howled anyway. It seemed a dagger in the neck still inflicted pain. Noted.

Olis must've recovered from the shock of the attack because he flicked his fingers at the beast and released a puff of amorphous silver light. Streaks of silver separated and pelted the monster. For a split second it seemed the spell had no effect—until the creature's chest glowed silver and exploded.

The dog-monster dissipated, leaving traces of an eerie blue light on the ground before the spot returned to a dull brown, as though the creature had never existed.

I stared at the empty space. "What kind of spell did you use?"

"A destructive one."

"Clearly."

"I've only used it once to break through a sealed tunnel."

I looked at him askance. "How did you know it would work now?"

He shrugged. "I didn't."

I contemplated the ground. "I don't get it. It looked

nothing like the monster at the theater, but neither one had blood."

"At least they could still be killed."

"Unless they weren't. Maybe it's self-preservation and they disappear when attacked, only to return later."

"What an uplifting thought," Olis remarked.

I compared the strange monsters. "One came from the sky and one came from below. What's beneath us?"

"It depends on the precise location. We should go back to the compound and have an artist sketch the beast while we can still describe it in detail."

I laughed. "You think I'll forget? That monster will haunt my dreams right beside his friend." I started forward. "I say we keep going and figure out why it was here. Let's locate your unusual something—unless that monster was it."

I heard the shuffle of the wizard's feet behind me. "I'm almost afraid to find out."

"I don't suppose your locator spell gave us an 'X' marks the spot."

"Not that precise, I'm afraid, but the appearance of the monster suggests we're on the right track, and that we're likely in search of the same object."

I paused in front of the gaping hole in the floor of the tunnel from which the monster had risen. I couldn't see anything except more dirt and rocks.

"This one could've come through the ward with its shaggy friend last night and bypassed the theater." I knew in my gut this wasn't another random monster occurrence. These creatures were after something and, whatever that something was, it was within this vicinity.

Olis hesitated. "What if there are more down here?"

"There are always more, Olis."

Always.

I continued forward and was pleased the wizard decided to join me. The fact that he was willing to put his neck on the line to defend House August territory was a promising sign. Then again, my mother once told me men were better at compartmentalizing. I'd been bewildered at the time, too young to understand, but maybe she was on to something.

At a certain point the tunnel narrowed and sloped further below ground. I'd never traveled this far beneath the city before. As we followed another bend in the tunnel, I heard the sound of music. *Sweet Child of Mine* by Guns N' Roses to be exact. A pre-Eternal Night song popular with humans toward the end of the twentieth century.

Finally, we reached the source of the sound—a CD player that had survived the Great Eruption. One boy bounced a tennis ball off the tunnel wall while the other played air guitar on a racquet. One of the boys noticed us and gasped. The ball bounced off the wall and rolled across the dirt, unclaimed. They looked no older than eleven. Their clothing was stained and torn and their faces were so covered in dirt that the boys looked like smudges against the shadowy background.

I held up my hands. "We're not here to hurt you." I cut a glance at Olis. "Show them your palms."

The wizard slowly raised his hands. He seemed stunned by the sight of these boys, which was strange to me. Everybody knew there were entire human communities that lived below ground, especially the Director of Security.

The boys turned and ran, swallowed by the darkness.

"Stop right there," a deep voice warned.

"Them or us?" I called.

"Boys are free to go," the voice rumbled.

Metal gleamed in the darkness. "Is that a shotgun?"

"No, it's a modified Taurus Judge. Can take your head clean off with one shot."

I nodded approvingly. "Nice."

Olis turned his head toward me wearing an incredulous expression. "You're complimenting the weapon about to kill you?"

I waved a hand at the gun. "What? It's a nice piece. I fired one once. Killed a hellhound. The small town it was terrorizing was very grateful, too. I ate cherry pie for a week straight." My stomach warmed at the memory of all that delicious pie.

"You killed a hellhound with the Judge? How?" the wielder of the weapon asked.

"For starters, don't try to take the head clean off with it. You aim for the gut and you're golden. That's where their heart is."

The man peeled away from the shadows and lowered the weapon. His clothes were slightly less worn and his dark beard was too bushy to determine the cleanliness of his face. "Who are you?"

"I'm Britt and this is Olis."

The man zeroed in on the wizard's wound. "You're hurt."

Olis touched the injury as though he'd forgotten it was there. "It will mend with proper treatment."

"What is this place?" I asked.

"You're at the entrance to the Hudson settlement."

Olis's head jerked. "The Hudson settlement? I thought you were a myth."

I glanced at him. "Seriously? Why?"

"Because I've never seen them with my own eyes."

"That's an interesting approach to the world around you, Olis. If you don't see it for yourself, it doesn't exist?"

"I realize how it foolish it sounds now that I hear you say it out loud," he admitted.

"We are very real." The man offered his hand. "I'm Jim, Southern Sentry."

I shook his hand first. Olis seemed less certain about touching the filthy appendage. For somebody desperate to restore the sun for humankind, he didn't seem particularly keen on making contact with them.

Jim pointed to the angry red mark on the wizard's forehead. "My husband can get you fixed up. He's one of our finest nurses."

I put a hand in front of Olis to stop him. "While we appreciate the gesture, first I think you should know who we are."

Jim's face flickered with uncertainty. "Why don't you enlighten me?"

Olis drew a breath. "I'm the Director of Security for House August."

To his credit, Jim remained calm. "Are you here in that capacity?"

"Yes and no," Olis replied. "We're not here for you or your people, if that helps."

"We're tracking monster activity," I added. "We killed one not far from here and another above ground. They seem to be searching for something, so we're hoping to find it first."

Jim licked his lips. "I see." His gaze flicked to me. "You're on the security team?"

"I was, but not anymore. I'm helping because..." How did I even complete that sentence? "The king is a friend."

Jim scoffed. "A friend? You realize you're not a vampire, right? Or maybe you can conjure a spell to look like one? I've heard of magic users who can get away with that.

Pretend to be one of them and reap the rewards. I couldn't keep up the pretense myself, but I understand their reasons."

"I don't pretend to be anybody other than myself."

"I can attest to that," Olis muttered.

"If you don't want us to enter the settlement, I understand," I said, "but I worry for your safety. If more of these monsters show up, you need to know how to protect yourselves."

"We've fought plenty of monsters down here, believe me," Jim said.

I shook my head. "Not like these."

Jim still seemed uncertain.

"The king isn't interested in foraging for food," I continued. "In fact, he's been investigating alternate methods."

Jim raised a skeptical eyebrow. "Alternate methods? What does that mean?"

"It means even if he found out there was an ample supply of human blood, he's not going to send a raiding party down here. His House has never sanctioned that kind of behavior and the king isn't about to start now. You have my word."

Jim nodded, appearing to reach a decision. "Come on then. Let's get you cleaned up. We can't send you back to the vamps dripping blood or they might need to hire a new head of security."

The 'settlement' was a miniature version of the city above. There were buildings, lampposts, and roads, although cars had been replaced by bicycles. As a child, I'd sometimes fantasized about being adopted by a human settlement. The ones I'd pictured in my fertile imagination didn't come close to the reality before me now.

"How did you get all the materials to build this?" I asked, still struggling to process the scene.

"It happened over time," Jim explained. "A lot of this started before I was born. Each generation has added more."

"Incredible," Olis breathed.

Bicycle bells jingled as they passed by and people called out in greeting to Jim.

"Aren't you supposed to be at the South Gate now?" a portly woman shouted.

Jim motioned to us with his elbow. "Got visitors."

The woman gave us an appraising look. "Paul's in the infirmary."

"I know. That's where we're headed."

We entered a squat building with a set of extra-wide doors. Jim waved to everybody he passed. In this setting, he seemed more like the mayor than a guard. He approached a counter where two women regarded us with fear in their eyes.

"Marcia, I need to bring this gentleman to Paul," Jim said.

"Room 102 is available," Marcia replied. Her gaze never left the suspicious visitors.

I'd seen the inside of my share of infirmaries and Room 102 was every bit as equipped.

Paul turned out to be remarkably tall for a human.

"Legend has it one of my ancestors was a giant," he quipped as he stitched up the wizard's gaping wound.

I decided to take advantage of our captive audience. "Has anybody made an interesting discovery lately? Maybe dug up a cool artifact?"

"What kind of artifact?" Jim asked. "Kids are digging up stuff all the time. It's a favorite pastime."

"Anything you haven't recognized?" I asked. "Our spell

indicates there's something down here those monsters might be after."

Jim and Paul exchanged glances. "You don't think...?" Paul began.

"I don't see why monsters would be after a thing like that," Jim said.

"It's the only recent find that I know of," Paul countered.

Jim scoffed. "It's only a hunk of junk."

To the untrained eye, maybe. "I'd like to see it."

Jim nodded. "I'll take you to her."

"Her?"

"Our daughter, Scout." He paused. "She was my sister's kid, but Paul and I adopted her parents died."

"Monster?" I asked.

He gave a long look. "That's how we describe them, but you might have a different opinion."

Vampire. Got it.

Once Olis's wound was dressed, Paul and Jim escorted us to their house. It was a small structure with only three rooms. The low doorway forced Paul to stoop to enter. The leather sofa was faded and worn but perfectly usable. Mismatched end tables flanked the sofa and there was a framed painting of a horse in a pasture on the wall behind them. A remembrance of a bygone era.

"Scout, sweetie," Paul called, "we have visitors."

A girl emerged from the doorway to the left. I placed Scout at about nine years old. Her hair was fixed in two braids, and she wore corduroy pants that were rolled up at the ankles. Bare toes peeked out from beneath the cuffs.

"Hey, Scout," I greeted her. "My name is Britt and this is my buddy, Olis. We heard you like to explore."

Scout cast a hesitant glance at her dads.

"That was one of my favorite things to do when I was young," I continued. "I'd go into the woods and dig holes and chase birds." The glory days, before I was expelled from the coven for my 'dirty' magic.

"Woods?" Scout echoed.

"I guess you've never seen the woods." There were no trees in the subterranean world. "Where I come from, there's an entire forest. We even kept an aviary. Do you know what that is?"

"Birds."

"That's right. We kept cardinals. Have you ever seen one?"

Shaking her head, Scout stared at me. "You're a witch."

"Smart girl."

"Not just smart," Jim said. "Gifted."

I twisted to look at him. "She has the Sight?"

Jim nodded. "She's one of our supernatural detectors. She senses when the monsters are in the vicinity. Inherited it from my side of the family. That's why I'm a sentry."

"Sweetie, can you show the nice lady the thing you found?" Paul prompted.

Scout disappeared into her room and returned with a large piece of metal cradled in her arms.

Jim was right. It looked like a hunk of junk.

With delicate hands, she placed it on the table. As useless as it appeared, the metal was in surprisingly good condition. Rectangular in shape and large enough to span a broad chest, it reminded me of a medieval breastplate from a knight's armor—if that knight were a giant.

"Did you see it sticking out of the dirt?" I asked. As dull as the metal was, it was still shiny enough to penetrate the darkness of the tunnels.

Scout shook her head. "I dug for it."

63

I frowned. "You were digging for fun?"

"Sometimes but not this time," Scout replied.

"Something drew you to that spot?" Olis pressed.

Scout nodded. "Energy."

"Scout knows where the ley lines are without looking at a map," Jim said, clearly proud of the girl's abilities. "She senses them."

"And you sensed that?" I motioned to the object on the table.

Scout nodded.

I looked sideways at Olis. "Do you think this is your mystery object?"

"It's a good bet."

"Where did you find it, Scout?" I looked at Jim and Paul. "Would you mind if she showed us?"

"That's up to Scout," Paul said.

The girl perked up. "Yes. I can take you there." She practically skipped out of the house.

Olis tucked the breastplate under his arm and together we followed her.

The underground city was like a maze. Some walls were created by buildings; others were created by dirt and rocks. It must've taken decades to create the city and its interconnected tunnel system. Some of the humans we passed seemed more feral than werewolves I'd met in the Southern Territories. Long, unwashed hair. Dirt-marked faces. Nails that resembled claws.

"Don't mind them," Scout said, noticing my reaction. "They won't hurt you."

"Why aren't they...?" I wasn't sure how to finish my question.

"Like us?" Scout interjected. "Some of them were.

64

These dwellers like donating too much. Dad says all the blood loss messed with their heads."

"Scout isn't supposed to be here on her own," Jim added with a pointed look at his daughter.

"I thought they were harmless," I said.

"They're unpredictable," he replied. "Just because they haven't hurt anybody so far doesn't mean they won't. I've seen a couple of them go nuts when they couldn't donate anymore."

"The vampires rejected their donations?" I asked.

He nodded. "At a certain point, their blood loses its flavor and doesn't provide the level of nourishment the vamps prefer. By then the people are addicted."

I tried to wrap my head around the concept. "They're addicted to *giving* blood?"

He snorted. "I know. Sounds crazy, right? But it happens. Once they're rejected, they waste away down here or get themselves killed up top in a desperate attempt to chase their high one more time."

I wondered whether House August was aware of the issue.

Scout turned a dark corner and picked up speed.

"Slow down," Paul called. "How can you even see where you're going?"

The offshoot was narrow with a low ceiling. Paul reached into his pocket and withdrew a bright flashlight.

Scout glanced over her shoulder with a delighted grin. "Almost there."

"What's the point of this area?" I asked, once we arrived at a dead end. "Why didn't people bother to finish the tunnel?"

"Oh, people didn't create this section. It was already here," Scout said.

"How do you know?"

She dusted off a carving on the wall. The images depicted a man walking at full height, then a little shorter with retracted legs and arms, and finally a butterfly.

"Vampires," I murmured. Of course. Before the Eternal Night, vampires had lurked in the shadows, out of sight. And some vampires, it seemed, had created a world of their own, underground and away from the sun's deadly rays.

"Ironic, isn't it?" Jim asked. "Vampires now control the city built by humans and humans have been relegated to the one built by vampires."

"It's like that story you read to me," Scout interjected. "The Prince and the Pauper."

Jim's expression clouded over. "Not quite. In that story, the prince and the pauper made a choice." He motioned to the tunnel. "You know you're not supposed to stray this far."

She lowered her gaze. "The energy drew me here, so I was exploring."

"You're an adventurer, huh? You and I have that in common."

The little girl beamed at me. "I find all sorts of treasures, but never anything like this."

"Do you know there are buildings filled with historic treasures like this one?" I asked. "They're called museums."

Gasping, she looked at her parents. "Can we go there?"

"It isn't safe, Scout. You know that," Jim said.

I frowned. "You've never been aboveground?"

Scout shook her head. "Not allowed. Too many of us leave and never come back."

"Or they become one of the wasted ones," Paul said.

I'd been under the impression that House August handled the blood situation in a more humane way, but I was beginning to question that belief.

Scout crouched in a dark corner of the tunnel and pointed to a hole. "I found it buried there."

Paul shone the light over a shallow hole that was about two feet in circumference.

"How did you dig it out?" I asked.

She held up her hands. "I would've used a spade if I had one with me. Sometimes I do." She laughed. "I don't think my fingernails had ever seen that much dirt."

"I don't think our bathtub had ever seen that much dirt either," Paul added with a twinkle in his eye.

I turned to Olis. "Do you think we should dig up the whole area and see if there's more?"

The wizard contemplated the tunnel. "I don't think that will be necessary." He held a hand over the ground, palm down, and whispered an incantation.

Scout's eyes rounded. "What's he doing?" she whispered in awe.

"I'm scanning the ground for abnormalities," Olis answered.

"You're allowed to do magic?" Scout tugged Paul's sleeve. "Dad, he's doing magic."

"He's allowed," I said. "He has special dispensation because of his job."

Scout moved to stand directly beside Olis. "How does the spell work?"

The wizard ignored her and continuing pacing the ground with his hand flat, using it like a metal detector.

She stared at me. "Can you do spells, too?"

"Afraid not. That's not how my magic works."

Her brow furrowed. "Then how does it work? Isn't all magic the same?"

Olis sniffed in indignation. "Certainly not."

I suppressed a smile. "Witches and wizards possess all

sorts of magic. I bet there are types of magic that exist that we haven't even discovered yet."

Scout's face brightened. "How would you discover something that's already inside you?"

"Don't you learn new things about yourself as you get older? Like maybe you only bounced a ball against the wall and thought that was all you could do. Until one day something happened that made you throw a ball thirty feet instead."

"I can throw a ball thirty feet, easy," Scout said with a note of pride.

"Sometimes we surprise ourselves," I said. "We're as much a mystery as the world is."

Scout broke into a wide, gap-toothed smile. "I like that. Means life will never be boring."

"My life has been many things, but boring isn't one of them," I agreed.

"You still didn't tell me what kind of magic you do," Scout pressed.

I ruffled her hair. "No, I didn't." With all the talk of blood and the wasted, I thought it best not to share my particular talent.

Olis finally lowered his arm to his side. "I don't sense anything else."

Scout's face crumpled.

"Your discovery is pretty cool all by itself," I told her. "You should be proud."

"That being said, I'm afraid we're going to have to relieve your daughter of her discovery," Olis said. "I can, however, offer compensation."

"From House August?" Jim spat on the ground. "No thanks."

Olis didn't argue. "As you wish."

"I'm sorry about your sister and brother-in-law," I said.

"Please don't start with the whole 'not all vampires' bullshit," Jim said.

I shook my head. "I wasn't going to. I've killed enough of them to know plenty of them are still nothing more than cold-blooded predators."

Jim's jaw tightened.

"I assume you can send communications aboveground," I said. "If you see any more unusual monsters or make any new discoveries, will you contact me?"

Olis's look of surprise made it appear as though he'd accidentally sucked a lemon. "Should it be you? What about your plans?"

"Not until this matter's been resolved."

"Mama didn't raise no quitter, eh?" Jim asked with a smirk.

My mother didn't raise me at all. No one did. But Jim didn't need to know my sad history. "Thanks for your help, everyone. We can find our way out from here."

"Are you sure?" Scout asked. "I know all the best paths."

I cut a glance at Olis. "I bet you do. I can't let you do it for free, though." I unsheathed one of my daggers. "This one's seen a lot of action."

Smiling broadly, she accepted the dagger and clutched it to her chest. "This is the best day ever."

I envied her enthusiasm. Maybe one day I could say the same.

Chapter Five

Olis and I returned to the compound in relative silence. Despite our possession of the metal fragment, we encountered no monsters.

"Tell the king we'll be in the debriefing room," Olis told the guards.

We arrived at the same room from the night before and Olis placed the metal fragment on the table.

"What do you think it is?" he asked.

"Breastplate for a giant's armor is my best guess."

"If that's the case it would be very old and I'm not aware of any giants roaming New York even before the Great Eruption." His fingers stroked the smooth center. "I've never seen metal like this. Have you?"

I shook my head. "Why would the monsters want it?"

"Perhaps it possesses untold power and it's simply drawing them like a moth to a flame."

"Maybe." Or maybe it was more than that. I looked at Olis. "You said you want to regain my trust. Tell the king about the wizards in the park. If there's a chance they're somehow responsible for the monsters..."

The wizard folded his hands in front of him. "I am aware of my responsibilities to the House, thank you."

"He needs to know."

"Part of my job is knowing how much information to share with His Majesty. The king is much too busy to be bothered by minor details."

"Details that happen to call your loyalty into question." I leaned forward and lowered my voice. "Did you really think your duties to this House wouldn't conflict with your extracurricular activities?"

"On the contrary, I knew it was inevitable."

"Are you afraid one of those wizards will rat you out? Is that why you haven't reported them officially?"

"No, they would never."

"What makes you so confident? Some kind of magic oath?"

"Because they know I would kill them before they got the words out," he said simply.

I recoiled as I viewed the wizard with fresh eyes. "You and I are more alike than I thought."

"Except you have certain weaknesses that I lack."

"Like what?"

"Concern for others, for starters."

I laughed. "You're in charge of security for the most powerful House in North America. I'd say concern for others is a priority for you."

He shook his head. "It's different. My concern is professional. It comes from the head. Yours comes from the heart."

I grunted. "I was an assassin, Olis. I hardly think my heart is the driving force of my personality."

"Remember what you said to the girl—to Scout—about making discoveries about ourselves?" He watched me expectantly. "I think that's one conclusion you'll reach eventually."

"You want to bring back the sun, Olis. If that doesn't show concern for others, then I don't know what does." Gods, I hated this feeling of ambivalence.

Alaric's arrival brought the conversation to an abrupt end. Guilt sank like a stone in my stomach. It didn't feel right to keep such important information from him. At the same time, I wasn't ready to throw Olis under the Big Apple bus. I needed more information and that would take more time to acquire.

"How's the debriefing?" Alaric asked.

"Waiting for you before we begin, Your Majesty," Olis said.

The vampire's gaze passed over the breastplate. "Your visit to the tunnels was fruitful, I take it?"

"It was, Your Majesty," I said.

He glanced at me. "You know you don't need to call me that."

"I know, but it's damn sexy."

The sexy head of House August stood at the head of the table. "So, what is it?"

"Best guess is the breastplate for a giant's suit of armor," I replied.

"Remarkably intact," Alaric observed. "Have we identified the type of metal?"

"Not yet, Your Majesty," Olis said.

His finger traced the sheet of metal. "It isn't any steel or iron I've seen before."

"What else is there?" I asked.

"Bronze," Olis said, "but it isn't that either."

I studied the breastplate. "Are you sure it isn't steel?"

"Not any steel I've encountered," Alaric replied.

I tilted my head. "Now I want to touch it again just to see if it feels any different."

"I went through a similar phase," Alaric remarked.

I shot him a pointed look. "We're not talking about actual breasts, Alaric." I cleared my throat. "I mean, Your Majesty."

Olis smothered a smile.

"How do you think such a fancy piece of metal got buried in the tunnels?" I asked. "Where would it have come from?"

Alaric swiveled toward Olis. "Check with the museums and see if anything is missing that matches this."

Olis bowed his head. "Right away, Your Majesty." He turned on his heel and exited the room.

"Is it possible to check the inventory of museums prior to the Great Eruption?" I asked.

Alaric searched my face. "You think this has been buried that long?"

"Maybe it was buried when the buildings were destroyed." Multiple museums suffered extensive damage as well as looting. It was possible this piece was lost during that chaotic time.

"It could even be from the destroyed home of a wealthy collector," Alaric mused. "Those records will be harder to trace. The question is why now?"

I tapped my stubby fingernails on the table. "Because a little girl named Scout found it. She's like a magic detector."

"In that case, this would be enchanted metal."

He made a good point. "Why would monsters be after an enchanted breastplate?" I asked. "It's not like they can wear it."

"Are you certain it's a breastplate?"

"I'm not sure of anything yet," I said.

73

Alaric rose to examine the metal from multiple angles. "Yes, I see what you mean."

"There's something else," I told him. "The monster that attacked us in the tunnel was bloodless, too."

"But the second monster was different from the first," he said.

I nodded. "The second one was like a hairless dog monster that dug its way into the tunnels."

Alaric perked up. "What about the serpent you encountered in the park? Did that have blood?"

I thought of the serpent's final moments. "Yes, black blood. It stank."

"Hmm. Anything else noteworthy that I can pass along to the research team?"

I regarded him. "You're starting to sound like a real king."

"You say that as though you're surprised."

"Not at all. I always knew you had it in you."

He smiled. "I'm glad one of us has confidence."

Another memory stirred, this one even less pleasant. "Have you heard of the wasted?"

He frowned. "People who drink to excess?"

"No, people who give blood to excess."

The vampire's eyes narrowed. "You mean until it kills them?"

"No, I mean until it destroys them to the point where they might as well be dead."

Hesitation flashed in his eyes. "I've heard tales of them. Where did you encounter them?"

"Doesn't matter. I think you should do something about them, though. They're almost unrecognizable as people."

"And you blame me for this?"

I recoiled. "Of course not, but I think it's the kind of thing you should be aware of as their king."

"There's a system in place..."

"A system that clearly isn't working for everybody."

"They were in the tunnels, weren't they? I didn't send you down there to analyze the conditions. I sent you to find out more information about the security issue."

"You didn't *send* me anywhere. Olis called me and I chose to help. I'm not beholden to your House anymore, remember?"

My whole body tensed as we glared at each other.

"I will worry about them when we no longer have a more pressing problem," he said in a measured tone. "Does that satisfy you?"

"Do I have a choice? I'm neither a king nor a vampire."

He exhaled. "Don't be like that, Britt. I have to prioritize. Hell, I'm still figuring out how to be king. Every time someone asks my opinion, I look over my shoulder for my father."

My body relaxed. "I'm sorry. I know this isn't an easy transition for you."

He reached for my hand across the table and squeezed. "You and I have been through a lot together. You've earned the right to speak to me as you wish."

My heart caught in my throat. This was the Alaric I loved. The one who spoke plainly and reasonably and with compassion. People say not to fall in love with someone's potential, but I did exactly that. No regrets.

Alaric's phone pinged and he glanced at the screen. "Finally! I have news. Your friend in the park was a bitie."

"A what-ie?"

"A bitie."

"Says who?"

"My research team."

I drummed my fingers on the table. "And what did they tell you about this creature?"

"You're right about the foul odor of its blood. Apparently, it reeks of a vat of rotten eggs." He raked a hand through his hair, a gesture I secretly loved.

"Do we think the serpent also came through the hole in the ward above the theater and ended up at the park?"

"But no one saw it en route to the park? A huge, two-headed serpent that growls?" Alaric shook his head. "The hole wasn't there long enough anyway."

"I'd like to know why these monsters in particular," I said. "Is someone sending them or are they being drawn here?"

He flicked the breastplate. "Maybe by this?"

I thought of the wizard we'd encountered in the Wasteland. The Monster Maze was his way of keeping vampires out of his domain and acting as the ruler of his own small kingdom. Unfortunately for him, his rule came to an end when he tried to kill us.

"Who would be powerful enough to tamper with a city-wide ward?" I asked.

"Maybe they're not that powerful, which is why they only took out a small segment."

"I don't know. That supernatural storm seemed pretty potent," I said. "Could be a team of magic users working for another House."

"Could be, but House Nilsson hasn't heard any rumblings of movement against us."

I frowned at him. "You don't seem overly concerned about a House war."

"I'm choosing patience. The last time we were in crisis, my mother rushed to judgment and that decision could've been catastrophic for our House." Alaric was referring to recent events involving the Pey, a group of primordial vampires that framed House Nilsson for the murder of King Maxwell.

"Do you think it's worth speaking to your mother about any of this?"

He shook his head. "She's in the Hamptons avoiding responsibility."

Like mother, like son—once upon a time.

"I'm glad you're still here," Alaric continued. "I trust Olis, of course, but having you here makes everything better."

I trust Olis. The words slammed into me. If Alaric ever found out that I was privy to the wizard's secrets and kept them to myself, he might never speak to me again. Even worse, he might believe me guilty of treason. The idea sickened me.

"Britt? What is it?"

I opened my mouth but couldn't bring myself to say the words. "Nothing, Your Majesty. It's been a long day."

"Then how about dinner with me? Might as well make the most of your continued presence in the city."

"You know I'm not one to turn down a free meal."

He broke into a grin. "I'll have your favorite wine. Who knows when your next chance to drink will be?" He started to type on his phone. "I'll tell the staff now and have Olis prepare a safe place for this metal until we learn more."

"You're very thoughtful, Your Majesty."

His gaze flicked to me. "You wouldn't have said that about me two years ago."

"Times change. *We've* changed."

"And I'm glad for it. I think about things I've done..." He stopped talking and shook his head. "I'm mortified."

"No sense clinging to the past. Learn what you can from it and move on."

"Wise words. My mother said something similar right before my coronation." He paused. "She likes you, you know."

I laughed. "She doesn't even know my name. She calls me Britta."

"Maybe before. She knows it now."

"And I'm sure she's thrilled you took up with a witch instead of a respectable vampiress."

He raised an eyebrow. "Nobody says vampiress."

"Apparently I do."

Olis returned to the room. "If you're finished, I can take this piece to a containment unit on the lower level, Your Majesty."

I snapped a quick photo with my camera phone. "Now you can take it."

"Maybe you should stay at the compound," Alaric said. "If there are monsters poking holes through the ward, it might be the safest place for you."

"If they can punch through the ward at the theater, there's no reason to think this place is safer than mine."

Olis and Alaric exchanged knowing glances.

"The compound has an extra layer of protection, doesn't it?" I should've known. "Fine. I'll stay, but only if there's a place for George." I wasn't about to leave the phoenix as fast food for visiting monsters.

"George is always welcome here. You know that," Alaric said. "He's a hero."

George had saved my life during the battle with the Pey. His sacrifice was how we'd discovered he was, in fact, a phoenix and not a pygmy dragon as previously believed.

I smiled. "You don't have to kiss up to him. He'll decide for himself when he's ready to accept you."

Alaric tapped an invisible wristwatch. "You're leaving the city, remember? The clock is ticking."

I shrugged. "You can't force these things. The phoenix has a mind of his own."

"Shall I have a room prepared for you?" Olis asked.

Alaric made a dismissive noise. "I'll have the house-keeping staff take care of it, Olis. You focus on matters of security. The gods know we have plenty to contend with at the moment."

Olis nodded. "As you wish, Your Majesty."

"See how respectful he is?" Alaric asked, once the wizard had left the room with the metal. "Why don't you try that?"

I laughed. "Have you met me?"

"You two are destined to become best friends, you know," Alaric joked.

"He's more like a grumpy uncle who gets pissy when you finish the last beer."

"I've never seen Olis drink beer." He stroked his strong jawline. "Funny. I never realized that before. My father always said you can't trust a man that doesn't drink." He blew a dismissive breath. "Then again, my father said a lot of nonsense."

I bit my tongue for now. A little more digging and I might be satisfied by the evidence in the wizard's favor.

True to his word, the king made the arrangements within a matter of minutes. A new quality to admire. The Alaric I knew had never been one to tackle a task. The vampire would ease his way in as though testing the heat of water or shirk the responsibility altogether.

A member of the housekeeping staff escorted me to my

quarters with a mild scowl. Although I recognized her, I didn't know her name.

"Everything okay?" I asked when she nearly elbowed me in the ribs in her haste to show me the contents of the closet.

The vampire bristled. "Certainly, miss."

"It's Britt. We've met before, haven't we? At one of the royal events?"

Her scowl deepened. "Where you served on the security team, yes, miss."

I was beginning to get the picture. I was no longer an indentured servant. In fact, I'd moved up in the pecking order. The nerve of me.

"I earned my freedom," I said. This vampire worked for a living wage. She didn't even know the half of my background.

She shut the closet door with a little too much force, causing the door to tremble. "Yes, I've heard the way you earned it, too."

"I assume you mean saving the king's life."

She smirked. "If you say so."

"You can resent me all you like. It doesn't change the fact that I have a nicer room in the compound than you do."

Her mouth drew into a tight line. "You have no right to be here. You're a..."

I folded my arms. "A what?"

"You know what you are," she seethed. "And yet here you are, to the manor born."

I pinned her with a hard stare. "Suck it up. You're a vampire. You should be good at that."

She left the room, but not without shooting me a final glare for good measure. I'd be sure to check my meals for spit. Before I could close the door behind her, Olis appeared in the hallway just outside the room.

"I think I might need my own security detail *inside* the compound," I told him.

He glanced in the direction of the maid. "I can't say I'm surprised. Vampires like Claudia feel the most threatened by us."

"Why?"

The wizard shifted his focus back to me. "Can you truly not understand? She's part of the elite species, yet she serves others. Right now, that includes you, someone she considers beneath her. How can she climb the ladder if other species begin to land on the rungs above her? It pushes her aspirations even further out of reach."

I sighed. "I don't see what's so great about the top of Vampire Mountain. The view is just as dark as it is anywhere else."

"Which brings me to the reason for my visit."

"I assumed you came with more towels." I waved a hand at the closet. "There are only about fifty in there. What if I run out?"

Olis surprised me by smiling. The wizard rarely found me amusing. "There's somewhere I'd like to show you tonight."

"Tonight? In the middle of a code red security risk?"

"I don't make the schedule for this. I have additional patrols and no monsters on the radar. Our visit will only take an hour or so, unless you choose to stay longer."

I didn't want to say too much in case we were overheard. If all members of staff felt like Claudia, they'd seize any opportunity to throw my ass into a pot of boiling water and watch me die a slow, agonizing death.

"What do you hope to gain from this?" I asked.

"I believe we've already covered that." He offered a slight bow. "I'll collect you promptly at eleven-thirty."

"Fine, fairy godfather, but my ride better not turn into a pumpkin before we get there or I'm filing an official complaint."

Chapter Six

Olis arrived at my room promptly at eleven-thirty. I'd enjoyed a sumptuous meal with Alaric and was relieved when he was called away on royal business. I didn't want to explain why I couldn't spend the evening in his company.

A black sedan awaited us at the corner. Olis opened the back door and motioned for me to enter. I slid into the back-seat and made myself comfortable in the plush leather seat. "I assume this isn't a House August vehicle." I peered at the tinted window between the front and back of the car. "Who's the driver?"

"Never you mind." Olis withdrew a vial from the inside pocket of his jacket. "You'll need to drink this first."

I stared at the glass of bright green liquid. "Sorry. Not a fan of kale juice."

Wordlessly he removed the lid and dangled the vial in front of my face. "This is a rule that can't be ignored, I'm afraid."

"Fine." I swiped it and drank.

"Don't be alarmed. You'll feel the effects rather quickly."

The world slipped out of view, leaving only an inky void. "What the hell, Olis?"

"More effective than a blindfold. I couldn't take any chances where you're concerned."

"I'm both indignant and impressed."

"Interesting. I didn't think you'd take it this well."

"You could've knocked me unconscious. Wouldn't that have been easier?"

"I need you to walk once we arrive at our destination. This way is more efficient."

"Are you suggesting you're not strong enough to carry me?"

"I'm not suggesting it. I'm saying it. You're slender but your muscles are deceptive."

"If the goal of this is to make me trust you, you're not doing such a hot job." I tried to focus on the movements of the car to memorize our path. Left turn. Two blocks. Right turn.

"Our route isn't direct, so there's no point attempting to memorize the path."

Damn wizard. He knew me too well.

After ten more minutes of driving, the car slowed to a complete stop and the door opened.

"Thank you," Olis said to the unseen helper.

Someone helped me out of the car and an arm looped through mine. "I hope that arm belongs to you, Olis."

He patted my hand. "It does, indeed."

"I hope we're not in Brooklyn. I have standards."

He snorted. "I can assure you we're not in Brooklyn." The edge of a vial touched my lips. "Drink this to restore your sight."

I slurped down the liquid and waited. Fuzzy edges appeared first, followed by dozens of moving shapes. Eventually the interior of a large, busy room came into focus. There was sawdust on the floor and wooden beams across the sloped ceiling. I didn't recognize the place.

"You should've told me we were going to a bar, Olis. I would've made room in my liver."

"The watermelon ale is a particular delicacy."

I smiled. "So you do drink beer."

"No, but I've listened to everyone rave about it enough times to know."

"You realize this is an act of treason," I said.

"Offering you watermelon ale? I know it isn't to everyone's taste, but I took you for someone with an adventurous palate."

I glared at him. "You know perfectly well what's happening at this bar, Olis, and it has nothing to do with flavorful beverages."

He perfected an innocent expression. "Oh? And what might that be? I'm merely here to enjoy a good game of darts with a few friends."

"And what will I be doing?"

His gaze sharpened. "Putting on a show of solidarity," he whispered. "Whether you like it or not, your freedom makes you fair game."

"Fair game? I'm not a pawn."

"No, I'd say you're more of a rook."

"Then I'm to be sacrificed? I really have no reason to cooperate in that case, do I?"

The wizard seemed startled by my response. "The rook is only sacrificed in certain endgames."

"What's wrong, Olis? Surprised that I know a little about chess?"

"Whatever you think you know, it isn't enough," he said vaguely.

I stared at the wizard. "You lured me here under false pretenses. This isn't about trusting you. This is about your stupid prophecy."

His expression hardened. "Despite appearances, I'm trying very hard to help you. If that doesn't instill trust, I don't know what will." He nudged me through the open doorway. "Now put on a happy face and don't interrogate anyone."

A group of people noticed Olis and greeted him with smiles and handshakes.

"I'd like to introduce Britt." Olis gestured to a pasty man who was best described as a walking jar of mayonnaise. "Britt, this is Elroy."

"Nice to meet you, Elroy."

The mayo's focus shifted to Olis. "This her?"

Olis nodded. "It is."

Elroy looked me up and down. "She doesn't look like much."

I crossed my arms and scowled at him. "We never do. That's why we're always underestimated."

"I, for one, wouldn't dream of underestimating you," a throaty-voiced woman said. Her red hair was styled in a chic, blunt cut and she wore a string of black pearls around her neck. "I'm Natasha. I've been dying to meet you, darling."

"A pleasure to make your acquaintance," I said.

The introductions continued as more people drifted over to join our growing group. There was no way I'd remember all the names, so I started to give them nicknames in my head. Aside from Mayo Man, there was Scarecrow, Sophisticated Lady, Too Tall for This Room, and

Grumpy Cat Face. Olis had faded into the background, whether on purpose or because he was shoved aside, I wasn't sure.

"And what do you think of the prophecy, little miss?" Elroy asked.

Little miss? Was this wizard for real?

"Right. The prophecy. I'm the point of a triangle. Lucky me, my favorite shape."

"How exciting for you," Natasha chimed in. "It's like watching history unfold right before our eyes."

"I doubt the people who witnessed the Great Eruption had such an enthusiastic response to watching history unfold," I shot back.

"What a time to be alive." Elroy raised a drink to his lips. "Has anyone offered our guest of honor a drink?"

The witches and wizards elbowed each other in their excitement to quench my perceived thirst. I didn't stop them. I was too happy to accept any free beverages passed my way, as long as they didn't blind me again.

"Walk me through this prophecy," I said, once I had a second pint in my hand. Gathering intel was thirsty work. "What happens? I burn the city to the ground and all the vampires with it?"

Elroy's brow creased. "You can conjure fire?"

"No, but my friend can." I sipped my beer. "He's a phoenix."

He cracked a smile. "Ah."

"A phoenix?" Craig echoed. "I thought they were extinct."

"So did I," I admitted. "Olis told me George was a pygmy dragon." I turned to search the crowd for Olis, but he was nowhere to be seen.

"You should take that as a good omen," Natasha said.

"That my dragon turned out to be a bird? What kind of omen is that?"

"A phoenix is rare and special, like you." Her smile turned flirtatious. It seemed Natasha might be interested in more than my prophecy placement.

"We've been working extensively with a variety of seers from around the globe and collecting their dreams to examine any commonalities," Elroy said, returning to my question.

"And you've connected enough dots to come up with this trinity theory," I said. According to Olis, there were three elements necessary for the return of the sun and my blood magic was one of them.

Elroy nodded. "Fascinating stuff, really. We believe the three of you represent the past, present, and future. That's why our symbol is the Ring of Eternity."

"Got a slogan, too? Come for the sun. Stay for the slaughter."

"The only ones to be slaughtered are those fangers," Craig replied. The bitterness in his tone left me in no doubt of his feelings toward our vampire overlords.

"Now Craig," another woman said gently. "Let's remember not everyone views vampires the way we do." She angled her head toward me.

"It isn't simply past, present, and future," a wizard named Milton chimed in. "The trinity also represents the mind, body, and spirit."

"Which one am I?" I asked, half joking.

"Which one do you think you are, dear?" the woman asked.

"Come now, Theresa," Craig interjected. "This one's the blood witch. She's obviously the body."

I didn't like the way he referred to me as 'this one' or

'the body,' like I was an object instead of a living being. Craig clearly had issues and I suspected some of those issues started with 'mis' and ended in 'ogyny.'

Natasha eyed me over the rim of her glass. "She's definitely the body."

Oh, wow. She wasn't playing coy at all.

"And what do you all expect me to do? How do we trigger this prophecy into starting?"

Theresa placed a hand on my arm. "Oh, sweet child. It's already begun."

"What made you decide to come tonight?" Elroy asked. "Olis said you rejected his proposal last time."

"I had nothing else to do. I'm stuck in the compound until...Well, it doesn't matter why." Olis wouldn't like if I revealed matters of House security, even to his den of traitors.

"I heard you were leaving the city now that you've brokered your freedom," Natasha purred. "I'm pleased to see those rumors were unfounded."

"Not entirely. I'm just moving more slowly than I expected." That was as much as I was willing to say on the subject.

Natasha inched closer. "I like moving slowly. I find delayed gratification so much more..."

"Gratifying?" I offered.

She broke into a wide smile. "See? We understand each other."

Craig's nostrils flared. "She's not here for you, Natasha."

Elroy maneuvered in front of my would-be seducer. "Tell us about your childhood. I'd love to know more about your background."

I faltered. "My childhood?"

"Elroy is the group secretary," Craig explained. "He keeps records on everything we learn."

Elroy's head bobbed. "And having you here at our disposal is an excellent opportunity to learn more. Perhaps there are salient details that will lead us to the other points of the triangle."

"I thought Olis said you knew one of the other points," I said.

"We have our suspicions," Elroy confirmed, "but we're not certain about anything, not even you."

"That makes two of us," I murmured, drowning my response in a mouthful of ale.

"I don't know how you've handled living in such close proximity to all those vampires," Theresa said with a visible shudder. "I've said the same to Olis. I'd be in flight or fight mode twenty-four hours a day and drop dead from the stress."

"I don't know. Vampires aren't all bad," I said.

The group stared at me as though I'd suggested we all convert to vampirism.

"Nobody is all good or all bad," I added.

"Britt is right. It's our actions that define us rather than our species," Natasha finally interjected.

Even though I knew she was only saying that to get into my pants, I was grateful for the support.

"The king is a vampire, but he's proven himself to be compassionate and brave and selfless." I brought the glass to my mouth to stop myself from yammering on about Alaric's virtues.

"King Alaric?" Craig asked in disbelief. "The vampire that slept with half of the city and then fled to the Southern Territories because his family knew he wasn't fit to rule? That king?"

Theresa shot him a warning look. "Steady now, Craig."

"What? We can gather together to overthrow vampire rule but slamming the king is a bridge too far?" Craig snorted. "I suggest you rethink your priorities, Theresa."

"And I suggest you mind your tongue in front of our esteemed guest," Theresa replied.

"If you'll excuse me, I need a refill." I pried myself away from the zealots and headed to the bar. I needed a break from all the vampire hatred. On one level, I understood it. On another level, I disliked the intensity of their negative emotions regardless of the target. It made me uncomfortable. Plus, there were three wizards at the bar laughing heartily. They seemed more my speed. Jovial and completely oblivious to the tension around them.

I squeezed between two of their stools and signaled to the bartender, who must've been watching me because he rushed straight over to take my order.

"You're her, ain't you?" the wizard to my right asked.

"If by *her*, you mean the prophecy princess, then yes."

He looked past me at his companion. "Is there a princess in the prophecy? I thought they was all witches."

I closed my eyes for a brief moment. "No, there's no princess that I'm aware of." Hell, what did I know? Maybe there was a princess.

"We'll buy her that drink," he told the bartender. He offered his hand. "I'm Frank, by the way. Good to meet you, princess."

I shook his hand. His skin felt dry and cracked, but the grip was firm and warm.

The wizard next to me belched. "You should visit the Archive Room," he suggested. "If you're a princess, that's the place to find out for sure."

"I'm not a princess. I'm very sure of my parents. I have

my mother's eyes and my father's nose and mouth." My father used to call me their little mosaic, before they discovered my special brand of magic, of course. After that I was their little monstrosity. Their little abomination. I wondered what they would think of tonight, where witches and wizards fought to stand close to me instead of shunning me.

"I inherited my father's Neanderthal brow," Frank said. "And Kurt here got his mother's chin with that sweet dimple."

Kurt was the belcher. He touched the tiny indentation in his chin. "You'd be surprised how many women are partial to a dimple."

"If only mine weren't on my ass," Frank lamented.

"What about me?" the third man dragged his stool closer to me.

Frank studied his companion. "Denny is the lucky recipient of his mother's charm, which is a good thing because he got his father's looks."

Denny took a good-natured swing at his friend's arm.

I accepted the drink from the bartender and sipped. I felt relieved to be among wizards more interested in beer than treason. "You guys don't seem as interested in disparaging vampires or waxing poetic about the prophecy."

"Oh, we only show up at these meetings for the booze," Denny said.

"And because of Natasha," Kurt added. He swiveled around to scan the crowd for the redhead. "She's worth a public execution."

"Are you two together?" I asked.

Frank and Denny burst into laughter.

"Didn't think so," I said. "She was hitting on me earlier."

Denny nudged his friend's shoulder. "See, Kurt? Never gonna happen."

"Maybe you should visit the Archive Room," I said. "It can tell you whether you have a chance with her."

Frank chuckled. "It isn't a room with fortunetellers."

Kurt gave me a curious look. "Have you never heard of the Archive Room?"

"No," I admitted. "Is it in the library?"

They looked at each other and laughed. "The library," Kurt repeated with amusement. "That's funny. Maybe they should relocate it to make it easier for people to access."

I could tell he was being sarcastic, but I didn't understand the joke.

"The Archive Room is a mystical place beneath the city where records of people and events are stored," Frank explained.

"He uses the term 'people' loosely," Denny added. "It covers everybody. Vampires, too."

Huh. "And what kind of information does this room of records include?"

"All kinds. You could find out about all my past deeds, if you were so inclined," Frank said. "No future deeds, though. The future remains unwritten."

I swallowed a mouthful of beer. "Good and bad past deeds? Or is this a history-is-written-by-the-winners situation?"

"I've never visited there personally, so I can't say for sure, but my understanding is any and all past deeds."

My curiosity was piqued. "Just the highlights or all the nitty gritty?"

Frank shrugged. "Not sure. I don't know who'd be interested in the nitty gritty."

I tried to picture a room large enough to store that much information. "Either way, that's a lot of knowledge in one place." I paused for another drink. "If one were interested in accessing these records, how would one go about it?"

"Oh, you can't just turn up with your library card," Denny said. "It's more complicated than that. They don't want residents abusing the system."

"Which they would," Frank added. "This is New York, after all. We'd abuse trashcans if there weren't butterfly patrols watching our every move aboveground."

"I know a guy whose cousin went there to get information to help someone with a legal dispute," Denny said. "He had to bring a piece of fruit as an offering."

"An apple," Kurt chimed in. "It has to be an apple."

"Like the Garden of Eden," I mused. Except the apple was what got Adam and Eve expelled rather than admitted. The symbol of knowledge was a nice touch though. "Where's the entrance?"

Frank's eyes widened. "You thinking of going for real?"

I shrugged. "I'm always in the market for information." And right now I had a lot of questions.

Denny squirmed on his stool. "I don't think they let just anybody in there, even with an apple. I think you need to be approved. Like I said, it's more complicated."

"Then I guess I'll show up with an apple for the teacher and see what happens." There were worse things than being turned away at the door.

"What kind of information are you interested in?" Frank asked. "Maybe we can help you."

Although I couldn't reveal too much about the current situation, I could still ask about my recent monster encounters. "I'd like to know more about a creature that I encountered in the Wasteland." A partial lie.

The trio recoiled. "You were in the Wasteland?" Denny asked.

"Oh, yeah. Battled monsters in the maze and everything."

"I think you really are the prophecy girl," Frank said in an awestruck tone. "What kind of monsters did you fight there?"

I described the one from the theater, as well as the one from the tunnel. "Know anything that fits the descriptions?"

Frank reeled off a list of names, all of which I knew and dismissed for one reason or another.

"Sounds like you know a lot about monsters," I said.

"He knows a lot of useless information, that's for sure," Denny teased.

The wizards clinked their glasses and laughed.

"What if I drew the creature?" I asked. "Do you think you could identify it then?"

"Ooh, yes. A game." Frank set down his glass and rubbed his hands together. "I love games. What do I get if I win?"

"How about I don't kill you? Does that work?"

The wizards stared at me with gaping mouths. When they burst into simultaneous laughter, I realized they'd tipped over into drunk territory. No matter. They still might be able to offer insight.

"She's funny," the drunker one said. He looked at me through heavy lids. "You're funny."

I curtsied.

I started with an easy one to test his knowledge, drawing the image on a napkin. If he couldn't guess this one, I wouldn't bother with the rest.

Frank tilted his head. "A hydra."

I flipped over the napkin and drew another image.

"Chimera," he said.

The other wizard squinted. "You sure? That looks very similar to my ex-wife and she was a real shrew."

Charming.

"Listen, Frank..." I began.

"My name's not Frank. It's Denny."

Okay, it seemed I might be a little tipsy as well. "Denny and Kurt, would you mind giving me and your friend a little space?"

Denny's mouth curved into a knowing grin. "Yeah, sure." He nudged his companion excitedly. "See you later, Frank. Let me know if you win the game." He offered an exaggerated wink before he vacated his stool.

Men were such simple creatures.

I sat on the empty stool. "Okay, Frank. You've dazzled me so far. Let's try another one." I drew the giant wolf-bear from the theater and turned it toward him.

Frown lines formed as he studied the image. "Yes, I remember this one."

"Remember? You've seen one?"

"In a library book years ago. They're known as the..." He cast a furtive glance at the rest of the room. "I should write it down."

"Because you can't pronounce it?"

"Because it's in the forbidden tongue."

He scribbled on another napkin and slid it across the counter to me.

Cor-Comedere.

"Heart-eaters?" I asked.

"You know your Latin."

"I know enough." I thought about the monsters I fought. "Do they eat hearts because they have no blood of their own and are trying to get some?"

Frank polished off his drink and slid the empty glass

across the counter. "Sorry, I don't know where the name comes from."

Were they a beastly version of more primal vampire like the Pey? But then how did it explain their attraction to the breastplate?

The breastplate.

One of the functions of a breastplate is to protect the heart. That couldn't be a coincidence.

"What else can you tell me about them? Why have I never seen one before?" Maybe they were native to South America and migrated to the coast over time.

Frank laughed. "That one's easy. Because they're mythical. They don't exist."

"The creature I fought in midtown was very much grounded in reality, let me tell you." Oops. The admission slipped out before I could stop it. Damn alcohol. The Inquisitor should switch to beer and stop torturing magic users to confess their illegal activities.

Frank started to choke, prompting me to whack him between the shoulder blades. "You're telling me you fought this creature right here in the city?"

"I have the scar to prove it." I rolled up my sleeve and showed him the red, angry lines that marred the surface of otherwise smooth skin.

The color drained from his face. "How many of these things do you think are here?"

"None, anymore," I said quickly. "All taken care of. Anything else you can tell me about them? You've been so helpful."

He shook his head. "Sorry. Too many cheap beers to be useful to you now. At this point I hope I can remember the way home."

That would help with my slip of the tongue. Hopefully he'd forget our exchange by morning.

I folded the napkins and placed them in my pocket. "Thanks, Frank. Fun game. You win."

He straightened on the stool. "What do I win?"

"Olis will pay your tab tonight."

Frank gazed at me with a drunk, dopey expression. "You really are a princess."

I slid off the stool. "Something like that. Have a good night, Frank."

I maneuvered through the crowd to find my handler. Olis was tucked in a corner, in the midst of an intense conversation with Elroy and Theresa. He looked tired around the eyes. Treason took a toll, it seemed.

"I volunteered your wallet at the bar," I told Olis.

The wizard didn't flinch. "The bartender has my card on file."

"Great. Are we finished?" I asked.

Olis glanced at his companions as though awaiting their approval. Who was in charge here anyway? No one seemed to take control of the evening's agenda. In fact, I remained unclear what the agenda even was, other than to display me like a trophy. The saving grace was the information I learned from Frank.

"The car's waiting for us." Olis reached into his inside pocket and withdrew another vial.

I stared at the bright green liquid. "Is that really necessary? If I wanted to turn you in, I wouldn't need to provide this location. The names and descriptions would be enough."

Theresa pivoted to face me. "On that note, why haven't you?"

"Well, for starters, I only met you tonight."

"But knowing your special relationship with the king, why haven't you mentioned any of this to him? Olis took a risk in sharing certain information with you, yes, but I'd like to know why his instinct prevailed."

I didn't know how to answer that. Although I felt a certain sense of loyalty when it came to Alaric, that loyalty didn't extend to all vampires. I was also curious about the prophecy and how I could possibly be involved. I was an outcast. A dirty blood witch. Yes, I possessed a rare ability, but it was the kind of magic that was reviled, not the kind of magic destined to topple regimes and tilt the world on its axis.

"I don't know," I answered honestly. "Olis and I have had our differences, but we're still more alike than not." I looked at the wizard for confirmation.

He slid the vial back into his pocket. "Good to see you, Elroy. Theresa."

"Nice to meet you both," I added.

"I'm sure we'll meet again," Theresa said with a nod.

I followed Olis to the exit and was grateful that no one intercepted us on our way out. "I know we're underground. I bet this place was some kind of speakeasy."

Olis maintained a passive expression.

"You haven't threatened me with life and limb if I tell the king. What's with the trust?"

My question prompted a sidelong glance. "If you do, you do. We'll cross that bridge if and when we come to it."

"That's a remarkably blasé approach for the Director of Security."

"I wear two hats, Ms. Death Bringer. The one I'm wearing right now is unrelated to the one I wear for House August."

"Yet you realize those two hats are diametrically opposed to one another, right?"

The wizard released a gentle sigh. "This again?" He pushed open the heavy wooden door. "People are complex and oftentimes contradictory creatures, Britt. I've accepted that about myself. I suggest you do the same."

Chapter Seven

The entrance to the Archive Room was accessible via a secret staircase in the Basilica of St. Patrick's Old Cathedral in the neighborhood formerly known as Little Italy, not to be confused with the Gothic Revival cathedral located on Fifth Avenue across from Rockefeller Center. The church itself was a relic of the past. No longer a religious sanctuary of the Catholic Church, it now served as a school for young vampires. Oh, the irony. Luckily school wasn't currently in session.

I was mildly disappointed the entrance wasn't in the more elaborate cathedral. Although most of the grand building uptown remained intact, its bronze doors and several stained-glass windows had to be replaced after a dragon attack prior to House August's resuscitation of the city. At least neither building had been burned to the ground like the churches in Britannia City.

My disappointment evaporated when I arrived at a walled, centuries-old cemetery. With a name like Death Bringer, you'd think I had a fascination with graveyards, and you'd be right. They were few and far between in the city, though. A cursory glance told me this cemetery was ancient and surprisingly well-maintained. I suspected there were a few donors to the school that prioritized preservation.

As much as I wanted to linger over the names carved in granite and imagine what their lives had been like, I had a more important task to accomplish.

Fingers gripped the top edge of my boot as I passed by a gravestone. To my credit, I didn't scream. I don't care how hardened you are, someone grabbing your foot from a gravesite is always going to yield a high creep factor.

"If you value your hand, you might want to release my foot," I said.

The creepy hand withdrew. I glanced at the ground to my left to see a bald, bearded vampire in a leather vest and matching pants crouched behind a gravestone.

"What are you doing down there?"

He remained in a crouched position as he looked up at me. "Sorry, thought you were someone else."

"Do I want to know?"

He offered a sheepish grin. "Probably not."

I pinned him with a hard look. "Is it consensual?"

His bald head gleamed in the darkness as it bobbed up and down. "Absolutely."

"In that case, carry on."

"I take it you're here for a different reason," he said.

"I'm looking for the Archive Room. Know anything about it?"

He pointed to the brick building a few yards in front of me. "You want the catacombs. Find Countess Annie Leary."

"She's like a tour guide or something?"

He grunted. "Yeah, or something."

"Thanks."

He gave me a sly leer. "Maybe when you're done in there, you could join us out here."

"You wouldn't want that." Smiling, I lifted my shirt to offer a glimpse of my dagger. "I like it rough."

He flicked his fang. "So do I."

I withdrew the dagger to give him a good view of the ten-inch blade. "Mine's bigger."

He scrambled back a couple inches. Message received.

I continued to the building and went in search of Countess Annie Leary. There was no sign of life. The name Annie bounced off the walls, so I stopped calling it. Red brick turned to white plaster, and I read the names inscribed on the arched doorways of the crypts. Finally, I found her, or at least I found her crypt.

Annie wasn't a guide. She was a marker.

I opened the door and crept inside. Darkness enveloped me. Somewhere in this tiny crypt was a hidden staircase to the Archive Room. The wizards weren't kidding about making the room inaccessible to the masses.

My hands felt along the walls, searching for anything that could pass for a door handle. What I hoped to avoid was a meeting with Annie herself. I wasn't overly fond of skeletons thanks to an unfortunate encounter when I was young and living on my own.

My hand touched a slight dip, so subtle that it could've passed for the dimple in Kurt's chin. I pressed it like a button. A tiny thrill shot through me when the wall slid aside to reveal a doorway. I still couldn't see for shit, but I entered all the same. Liam was always pestering me to carry a flashlight. Maybe next time I'd listen.

My foot reached empty air and I lowered it to a step. Success! As I descended the staircase, I lost count of the number of steps. At some point I reached a landing where a shiny metal door awaited me. I pressed a red button and the door slid open.

"An elevator?" Alrighty then.

I stepped inside and examined my options, which was easy because there were none. The doors closed and the elevator started to move. My stomach dropped along with the car. When the doors finally opened, I stumbled out, praying I didn't vomit. My offering was meant to be an apple, not a regurgitated meal.

I entered a small lobby. If there were archives here, they were invisible. A lone woman sat behind a clear and chrome desk. Her brown hair was styled in an updo reminiscent of a Greek goddess, and she wore a white, flowing dress that brushed the tops of her golden sandals. Hell, maybe she was a goddess. There seemed to be one of everything else. Why not archives?

She rose to her feet to greet me. "Welcome."

"Hi there. I'm looking for the Archive Room."

Smiling, the godly woman splayed her hands. "Congratulations. You found it."

"Perfect." As the wizards had instructed, I produced a bright red apple from my pocket. She studied the offering with a critical eye, and I was glad I'd selected one without any noticeable bruises.

"Gala?"

"Honeycrisp."

Her face relaxed. "I'm Irene. It's nice to meet you." She plucked the apple from my hand and motioned me toward a second elevator. "As it happens, I have space in the schedule now."

I entered the elevator and the doors screeched closed. The sound didn't give me much confidence in the equipment.

"Seems like a complicated process just to get information," I told her.

"Information is power, sweetling. You're fortunate to be here at all. Not everyone is permitted."

"Even if they bring an apple?" I asked.

She cut me a look. "Even if."

"So I could get turned away at the door?"

"Oh, no. The elevator would've already spat you out if you were to be denied entry. You're in." She patted my back. "Well done, you."

"What's the criteria for admittance?" It wasn't as though I was a paragon of virtue. If I was allowed in, who exactly was kept out?

"No clue. I only know the outcome. I used to have a theory, but not sure if it bears repeating." The elevator slowed to a crawl as it descended to greater depths.

"I'm interested to hear it."

Irene drew a breath. "I used to think it was a King Arthur situation, like only someone worthy could enter."

My admittance blew that theory out of the water. "And now?"

"Now I think it might be unrelated to worth. Too hard to determine. So I think it's more about your reasons for seeking information. The room knows if you're here for selfish purposes."

"If it helps, my reason for being here isn't about me, not directly anyway."

She cast me a sidelong glance. "And you're not here to gain information to use against someone for nefarious purposes?"

I shook my head. "No bribery or extortion intended."

"That squares with my theory." The speed of the

105

elevator started to pick up. "I hope you don't suffer from motion sickness," she said.

"Oh, I already..."

The car dropped. It was less of an elevator now and more of a zero-gravity ride. I gripped the handle on the side of the car and clenched my teeth so as not to bite my tongue. Irene looked almost serene as the car plummeted toward the earth's core.

Our rapid descent slowed as we approached the bottom, and I was relieved when the car came to a complete stop. The door opened and I tumbled forward, dry heaving.

"There's a bucket to your left should you need it," Irene chirped. She sounded remarkably cheerful for someone who handled vomiting visitors on a regular basis.

My stomach got its act together and I straightened. "I'll be fine."

Irene pointed ahead of us to a pair of enormous iron gates. "The archives are through there. When you hear the bell, that means your time is up. Look for the exit signs and they'll lead you back here, although some people find the spool helpful." She inclined her head to the right, where I noticed a wicker basket filled with colorful spools of thread.

I laughed. "I don't think that'll be necessary."

"Suit yourself." Irene pulled a lever on the wall and the gates clanked as they opened. "If you want to see how the system works, you can find my tablet in row I for Irene. My life is an open book, so I don't mind using myself as an example."

'I' for Irene seemed simple enough.

"I hope you find what you're looking for." As she turned toward the elevator, she seemed to remember something. "Oh, and if you see a large beastie, don't be alarmed. She lives down here. Just make sure you don't feed her. She doesn't have the best track record in determining which is food and which is the person offering the food." She wiggled her fingers over her shoulder. "Toodles."

"Bye."

"No, that's the name of the beast. Toodles. We call her the Archive Room mascot."

I didn't have any food with me, and I couldn't decide whether that was better or worse in the case of Toodles. I'd have to take my chances.

I sallied forth and stepped through the open gate. The 'room' was nothing like I expected. Shelves stretched in every direction as far as the eye could see. How was I meant to find anything without the wisdom of the Dewey Decimal System to guide me? Such an underrated cataloguing system.

I turned back to ask Irene for assistance, but the gates were already closed behind me. Now that I saw the interior, I began to regret not picking up a spool of bright thread.

I chose the path directly in front of me to get the lay of the land. If I kept walking, maybe I'd find a directory. If I could make it through the Monster Maze in the Wasteland, I could handle a room of records. An ancient and mystical room, yes, but still—records, not monsters.

Unless you counted Toodles.

I tried not to think about the archives mascot.

I pivoted to the shelf on my right at eye level. All information here had been recorded on indestructible tablets of brass and iron, which seemed impractical from my point of view, but hey, the gods didn't consult me.

I tried to prioritize my search. It could take me all day to find one tablet and I didn't have time to waste. I considered searching for a tablet devoted to 'ancient breastplate,' but I thought it wiser to start with 'bloodless monsters.' Too bad there wasn't an index to cross-reference.

I walked along the row and eyed the names on the tablets. I couldn't believe how much information was stored here. Did House August know such a place existed within their territory? Arguably the mystical Archive Room existed outside of our reality and, therefore, didn't belong to the vampires. I wasn't sure they would agree with that interpretation though. Either way, it seemed there were restrictions in place to keep the information sacred.

I located the section for 'B' and tried to unearth information on bloodless monsters but that proved fruitless. I moved on to 'C' and searched for Cor-Comedere. I figured if there was no entry I'd try heart-eaters next.

To my great relief, there was an entry.

There were no pages like a book, and I wondered how I'd be able to access the information.

I needn't have worried.

The moment I touched the tablet to remove it from the shelf, the information flooded my system. Heart-eaters are supernatural creations, which explained the absence of blood despite my ability to kill it. It also made sense in light of the supernatural storm that had accompanied its arrival.

Cor-Comedere can only be created and controlled by a god or goddess. Very interesting. What the tablet didn't reveal was which deity created the one I encountered.

"There's a flaw in the system, Irene," I grumbled.

There was also a section of related terms, including 'keelut.' Once I was satisfied, I'd absorbed all the knowledge I could, I returned the tablet to the shelf and headed over to 'K' to see if the term was relevant in any way.

The term turned out to be extremely relevant. A keelut was described as an oversized hairless dog, which I instantly recognized as the beast that attacked us in the tunnels. They lived in the earth itself. More importantly, the monster was considered a spirit, which was the reason it was bloodless and the reason Olis was able to destroy it with a spell, although according to the tablet, we could've also beheaded it.

Another related term bubbled to the surface of my mind —Hudson Island. The term had been mentioned in the other tablet as well, but I'd dismissed it as irrelevant. Now I wasn't so sure.

I tried to sift through all the information in my head and memorize the salient details before I left. I had a feeling the Archive Room didn't hand out frequent visitor cards. This was likely my only chance to access the information contained here. The realization prompted me to add a quick search for breastplates.

As I passed by a row of tablets in 'B,' a glint of metal caught my eye. I wasn't sure why, given that every tablet in the room was made of metal. I took a step backward to examine the tablet more closely.

Britt Miller, see also Death Bringer, Britt the Bloody, Britt the Blood Witch.

A lump formed in my throat. Was this really *my* record? I stared at the tablet for a full minute, debating whether to access the information. It seemed silly to bother. After all, I'd lived through each recorded incident. I didn't need to learn anything.

And yet.

I remained rooted in place, unwilling to walk away without sneaking a peek. What if it was inaccurate? Was there a form for disputed information?

I pulled the tablet off the shelf. As with the others, the moment my hands made contact with the metal, the information poured into me and my mind struggled to organize the data into digestible chunks. George was there—identified as related content. Nice.

Not all of it was nice, though.

Moments revealed themselves like a mental slideshow. My mouth turned to cotton when I saw the vampires I'd killed. I knew I'd been responsible for many deaths, but seeing them all at once like this...My stomach churned with regret and revulsion.

I thrust the tablet back on the shelf to ease the information overload. My mind calmed and my breathing slowed. What an ugly truth to confront. I mean, I knew there was blood on my hands. I'd done what I needed to in order to survive, at least that was the line I fed myself each and every time. Maybe I was mistaken. Maybe I could've chosen a different path. Or if I couldn't survive any other way, maybe I didn't deserve to live. I'd chosen indentured servitude that day, but maybe death would've been the right call. Too late now. I'd made my choice and here I was. At least I was trying to do better. I wouldn't describe it as atonement, but I was fighting for a cause greater than myself. This wasn't about my survival—I could leave New York right now and let the city fend for itself.

I was fighting for those who couldn't fight for themselves.

Part of me wanted to take the tablet so that no one else could ever bear witness to my transgressions. I suddenly understood the need to make the tablets indestructible. It wasn't always a pleasant stroll down memory lane. The archives were like mirrors, and not the amusing funhouse kind. I was forced to view my actions through a dispassionate lens and see them for what they truly were.

Desperate.

Depraved.

I'd given myself a free pass to do harm because harm had been done to me. Seeing it laid out before me now was eye-opening. And awful.

I tore myself away from the tablet and ran.

As my footsteps pounded the floor, I heard what I thought was an echo, until I realized it was a second set of footsteps.

Then I heard a low growl.

Toodles.

And here I thought I'd escape the beast's notice. Running like prey wasn't my smartest move.

I glanced over my shoulder to see a pair of eyes glittering like two emeralds in a cave. If I slowed down, I'd have to fight. I didn't want to fight the beast. So much blood had been spilled by me already.

However, blood didn't always have to be *spilled*, not when there was another method available to me.

I ground to a halt and spun on my heel to face the beast. Powerful shoulders broke through the black wall, followed by a long, elegant body, over eight feet in length. Humans might mistake the creature for a mixed-breed panther and tiger on steroids, but I recognized the creature for what it was.

A pozuzo.

Before the Great Eruption, people had identified a mystery feline known as a striped jaguar. The pozuzo were the larger, stronger, much scarier descendants.

I adopted a soothing tone. "Hey, Toodles."

The beast's whiskers twitched, as though surprised by my familiar greeting. Maybe I could bypass magic and try to appeal to the creature the old-fashioned way.

"I don't want to hurt you," I said gently. "I only want to find the exit and leave you in peace."

The beast snarled, whether expressing disbelief or displeasure, I wasn't sure.

"I don't have any food. Sorry about that."

A low growl emanated from Toodles, causing the hair on the back of my neck to rise up. She could've pounced by now. What was stopping her?

An idea occurred to me. Toodles could've easily left the Archive Room if she wanted. Forced her way into the elevator and rode to freedom. Food had to be scarce, which was the reason she pestered—and sometimes ate—visitors. So what kept her here?

I regarded the beast. "Why do you stay?"

Toodles kept her steely gaze fixed on me.

There was only one thing this place had to offer and that was information. I surveyed the endless rows of records. "Is there something you want to know?" The pozuzo had originated in South America, which begged the question—what was she doing in New York? "Do you want information about yourself?"

Toodles stopped growling and her whiskers twitched.

The wizards had said the archives contained the records of people and events, but what if they included information about all living creatures? Maybe Toodles couldn't access it because it was for a selfish purpose, although I wasn't convinced that rule applied to creatures like her.

"Tell me what you want to know."

I didn't possess the magical ability to communicate with animals. I knew such a skill existed, although it was rare. One of the witches in the Lancaster coven could do it. She was prized for her ability, as though she'd chosen it herself rather than having the good fortune to be born with it. I pushed the resentment aside and focused on the beast.

"You've lived here all alone, with limited access to food. There must be a good reason. I don't think it's that you're shy or scared." If anything, Toodles looked sad. I could tell by her limited number of stripes that she wasn't old. Young and alone in a strange place. No family.

And suddenly I knew.

Like many orphans, Toodles was searching for her family and she was smart enough to know the answer was hidden somewhere in this endless room.

"Toodles, would you like me to find information about your family?"

The beast rose to her full height and roared.

I took that as a yes.

There was nothing under 'T' for Toodles. Where else could I look? It could be anywhere. Then I remembered the one I noticed for George. The tablet had been close to mine, so it seemed the one for Toodles might be in close proximity to people with whom the beast was within close proximity.

Irene.

I hurried along the rows in search of row I. Igor. Ivan. Nope. I backed up to find Irene and retrieved her tablet. The beast watched me from the end of the row.

Preparing for the onslaught of information, I clutched the tablet to my chest and closed my eyes. Images assaulted my mind. I scanned my mind for related content.

And there she was.

I saw two beasts very much like Toodles. Okay, I could've done without the mating scene. Obviously Toodles wasn't the product of a virgin birth, but still.

I released the tablet and once again adjusted to the

gloaming. Toodles waited at the end of the row, stretched across the floor like a large and lazy barricade.

"Your mother was called Nimble and your father was Mateo. They met in South America, which is where you were born. There were so many monsters, they felt it was unsafe to raise you there. They decided to come to North America, where they believed you'd have better access to food. They intended to live out west because there are fewer people there, but they...didn't make it. Your mother contracted a disease and your father died hunting." I figured she knew the rest, that she was adopted by a group of panthers on their trek eastward.

Toodles seemed to understand.

"You're a survivor, Toodles." I crouched down to place a comforting hand on the beast's paw. "Like me."

At first, I thought the beast was emitting another growl, until I realized the sound was more like a running motor. She was purring.

"I'm headed to the elevator now," I said. "I can't promise you a rose garden, but I know a place with plenty of food and space to roam freely. What do you say—would you like to rejoin the land of the living?"

I didn't wait for a reply. I started toward the exit sign. A few steps later I felt the beast's presence beside me.

The Archive Room may have lost a mascot, but the rest of the world was about to gain a marvel.

Chapter Eight

"Where do you expect her to live?" Alaric gazed at me with a combination of annoyance and wonder.

I stroked the top of Toodles' head. "Look at the size of her. Wherever she wants, obviously."

Alaric rubbed his face, a sure sign of agitation. "Can she breathe fire?"

"Don't think so."

"She might make a decent companion for you on the road."

"She's traveled enough. She needs a home."

Alaric gave me a pointed look. "Hello, kettle."

I covered the beast's ears with my hands. "She's only little. Let's not argue in front of her."

Alaric rolled his eyes. "Fine. She can stay in the compound. House August is in need of a house cat. We might as well have the largest option available."

I released Toodles and threw my arms around the vampire. "You big softie. I knew you'd cave." I planted a sloppy kiss on his cheek. It wasn't my style to be overly affectionate, but I was so thrilled for Toodles.

"What about the breastplate?" he asked, as I unhooked my arms from his neck. "Did you learn anything more about it? The kind of metal it is or maybe its owner?"

I cringed. "I might have gotten a little distracted and left without researching that one." I straightened. "But heart-eaters and keeluts are important intel and I think Hudson Island might be the key to learning why they're showing up here now."

According to records, Hudson Island sprang into existence during the Great Eruption. Other islands had surfaced around the globe, but this was the only one close to New York. The island was small, only about four miles squared, and ten nautical miles off the mainland. As far as we knew it was uninhabited. House August sent a weekly swarm of butterflies to patrol the area, but there'd been no reported incidents there—ever. The Archive Room, however, suggested a different story.

"If you can set me up with a boat, I'll go today," I told him.

Alaric balked. "In person? Why? I'll simply send a patrol team."

"And alert whoever or whatever is there? No, if these bloodless monsters are using the island as a launching pad and we need to fight, then we need the element of surprise."

"One security sweep can give us the intel we need to prepare."

"Too risky," I insisted. "I know how your patrols operate. Those brightly colored wings are like beacons in the night."

Alaric smiled at me. "I'm the king, yet you presume to tell me how to run my team."

"Don't play the king card."

He inched closer. "Oh, I'm not. Your commands are very hot." His lips brushed against my cheek, causing an internal meltdown of my defenses.

Reluctantly I nudged him away. "Now isn't the time. There's an island to explore."

"I'd much rather stay here and explore." Alaric's soft kiss on my neck was far more distracting than any tablet in the Archive Room.

Toodles whined and turned away.

I edged away from him. "See? You're embarrassing your new mascot."

Relenting, Alaric heaved a sigh. "You can't go to the island alone. It's too dangerous."

"Well, you can't go. You're the king. You have a responsibility to your subjects to stay safe. Where does that leave us?"

"I'll send a team with you."

"Of vampires?" I laughed. "You send me to a remote island with vampires and they'll make sure I never return."

"They take orders from me. They would never…"

I folded my arms. "They would try, and I would kill them, or they would leave me there. Either way, it's a distraction from the actual goal."

"Duly noted. I don't want to hire an external team. I'd rather keep this under wraps and not cause a city-wide panic." He looked thoughtful. "What about Liam?"

"You want me to take my friend with a fondness for explosive devices?"

"Worked in our favor last time."

"That was different."

Alaric cocked his head. "Why? You needed his help and he provided it."

"There were innocent children to consider in the Wasteland. Liam is an engineer. He has no reason to put his life on the line for..." I trailed off.

"Go on, Britt. You can say it. For a city of vampires."

I exhaled. "You can't blame him."

"I wasn't expecting him to do it for vampires. I was expecting him to do it for you." Strong arms encircled me. "I need you safe, Britt, and I trust Liam to help with that."

I rested my head on his chest for a brief moment, craving the closeness. "I'll ask him."

"Good. I'll arrange transport." He paused. "The Archive Room sounds like an amazing place. I can't believe I didn't know about it."

"This city is full of surprises."

Transport came in the form of a dinghy. Liam and I stood at the dock at the Battery and stared at the small vessel built for two medium-sized occupants, or one very large one.

"Are you sure he doesn't have a death wish for us?" Liam asked. "This barely qualifies as a boat. How are we supposed to survive a sea monster attack?"

"I think the size is for our benefit. It's too small to be noticeable by any threats."

"Speaking of too small to be noticeable, where's George?"

"I didn't tell him where I was going."

"Why not? This seems like the perfect situation for a phoenix friend."

"I didn't want to endanger him."

"Oh, sure. Let George stay safe and sound but walk old Liam straight into the lion's den."

"George will follow me anywhere. It isn't fair to take advantage of that."

Liam gave me a critical look as he tossed his backpack into the boat. "You owe me for this."

I climbed into the dinghy and patted the space in front of me. "All aboard."

Reluctantly Liam boarded the small vessel. "Where's the motor?"

I lifted an oar from the bottom of the dinghy and handed it to him. "Here you go."

"And the hits keep on coming."

"Oh, please. You're strong."

He pointed to the choppy water. "See those waves? Makes it harder to row."

"A motor would be more likely to summon a sea monster. The oars are safer."

"And slower." He surveyed the bottom. "Where's the other one?"

I located the other one next to my foot. "Do you want to take the first shift or shall I?"

"I'll do it," he grumbled.

Based on current conditions, I estimated it would take us two to three hours to reach the island. Liam could row for ninety minutes and then I'd take over until we arrived.

We set off into the darkness. Once upon a time, ferries came in and out of the harbor filled with visitors to Staten Island and the Statue of Liberty.

Those days were long over.

"This is the short end of the stick," Liam complained half an hour later. "Why didn't the king just send a butterfly patrol?"

"Because I told him not to."

He grunted. "I like how the king takes orders from you now."

"We're going for more than monsters. I'm hoping we get answers, too."

He nudged the backpack with his foot. "I came prepared for monsters."

"Me, too." Knowing the creatures might be bloodless, I packed an array of weapons, although not so many that we'd sink the boat. It was a delicate balance.

"You know, Britt, for someone leaving town, you sure are around a lot."

"This is more important."

"Why? Because the king deems it so." He blew out a breath as he continued to row.

"There's a looming threat, Liam. What kind of person would I be if I up and left?"

His gaze met mine. "A survivor."

"More like a selfish coward."

Liam groaned. "You've got to be kidding me."

"No, I really would be a selfish coward."

"Not that." He pointed behind me. "That."

I turned to peer at the surface of the black water where two small ears on a large head emerged from the depths. A pair of round eyes focused on us.

"Is it friendly?" Liam whispered.

"Not sure yet." Although in my experience, nothing that lived in the water was ever friendly.

The eyes moved closer to the boat. I reached into my bag of tricks and felt around for the right weapon, which was hard to determine without knowing which monster it was.

As fast as Liam rowed, the monster managed to stay on our tail. "I can't shake it."

"Just keep rowing. Let me deal with our barnacle." I twisted to face the monster. Its hippopotamus-like head was now visible. "It's an aptu."

Liam gawked at the water monster. "Not the prettiest flower in the garden."

I'd never encountered one personally, but I'd heard tales of them over coven campfires in Lancaster. "They resemble hippos, but they're much bigger and much deadlier."

"No wonder sailing fell out of fashion."

I observed the aptu as it continued to swim after us. "I can't tell if it's hungry or lonely."

"I'm not interested in helping it with either of those options."

"Fair enough." I tried to remember any important facts I might've learned about the monster. Nothing sprang to mind.

"Can you use your blood mojo?" Liam suggested.

"I don't want to agitate it for no reason. It seems content to swim near us."

"What happens when we reach the island?"

"Hopefully it gets bored and swims away before then." I didn't like killing monsters for the sake of it. If I was threatened or attacked, fine, but this creature seemed docile.

"Speaking of bored, it's your turn to row." Liam thrust the oars toward me.

"Then it's your turn to keep an eye on our friend."

"I can do that." He looked past me. "Where'd it go? I don't see it."

The boat rocked and my stomach clenched when I realized what was happening.

Closing his eyes, Liam gripped the sides. "It's under the boat, isn't it?"

I didn't get a chance to answer. The boat lifted up, away

from the surface of the water. I let go of the oars. There was no point in rowing when the oars no longer reached the ocean.

"I thought we might die on the island. I didn't anticipate dying before we get there," Liam said.

I perked up.

"You seem awfully chipper about it," the werewolf accused.

"I don't think it's trying to hurt us. Just the opposite. I think it's trying to help us."

Frowning, Liam looked down. "You think it's ferrying us to the island?"

"That's exactly what I think."

Liam glowered. "Figures it shows up after my turn to row."

A cluster of clouds came into view, distinctive for their uncharacteristic red glow.

I pointed. "Jackpot."

The werewolf followed my gaze and winced. "A jackpot is a good thing. That looks ominous."

"It means we're headed in the right direction." Although I couldn't yet see the island through the haze of darkness, it was likely directly below the angry clouds.

As we approached the red glow, the dinghy unexpectedly dropped back to the surface of the water with a splash. I caught a final glimpse of the aptu as its head submerged.

"Thank you," I called, waving.

"Doesn't it make you nervous?" Liam asked.

"It carried us this far. I don't think it plans to hurt us."

"No, I mean, how scary is this island that even the water monster doesn't want to be close to it?"

"Good point." I picked up the oars and resumed rowing. At least I'd be well-rested for any impending monster fights. "If there's a hairless dog monster, you need to behead it. If it's a wolf-bear, you can kill it any which way."

"With kindness?"

"If only. I used a dagger through the eye."

"A delightful image. Thank you for that."

We sat in silence for a few minutes as I focused all my energy on rowing.

"Land, ho," I finally said.

Liam looked at me askance. "Water, bitch."

Shaking my head, I pointed. From this distance, the island's silhouette made it look like a pile of floating rocks. No trees, of course.

The wind picked up as we attempted to approach the island.

Liam straightened. "Did I see lightning?"

A boom of thunder answered his question. The stormy weather seemed concentrated above and around the island. There was no sign of rain, which would make our investigation somewhat easier.

We navigated past a steep cliff to find an easier place to go ashore.

Liam unzipped his hoodie. "Want me in wolf form for this part? It might be good for tracking."

"I have a feeling there won't be any tracking required." The monsters I'd met so far weren't subtle and they weren't hiding.

We guided the boat to shore and climbed out to pull it safely on land. The beach was comprised of more rocks than sand. It wouldn't make for easy walking.

"I could carry you on my back," Liam said, as though sensing my apprehension.

"Since when am I too frail to climb rocks?"

"Thought you might want to save your strength for the return journey. I have shifter muscles in my favor."

"I'll be fine, but thanks."

"Just so we're clear, it wasn't a comment on your gender, or your species."

"I know."

"Because I've seen you tear apart enough monsters to be a teensy tiny bit afraid of you."

I stopped walking and looked at him. "You're afraid of me?"

He held his thumb and index finger a hair's breadth apart.

"I don't think it's healthy to be afraid of your best friend, Liam. In fact, I'm mildly offended."

"Oh, gods. I've offended you. Now I'm definitely scared."

I folded my arms and glared at him. "Are you mocking me? Maybe you missed the part where I'm a favorite of the king."

A smirk emerged. "You really are the cherry on his blessed life sundae."

I punched his arm. "Stop. You're making me blush."

"I thought that was the job of His Majesty."

"You're lucky we're on a deserted island."

Without warning, the earth trembled beneath our feet. A shiver shot through me.

Liam's eyebrows inched up. "You were saying?"

I motioned to zip his lip. Our primary advantage would be the element of surprise, assuming, of course, that the threatening sound we heard wasn't directed at us.

We grabbed our bags and headed inland. There were plenty of boulders to use as shields along the way should the need arise.

"Are you sure you don't want me to shift?" Liam whispered.

I shook my head. Werewolves tended to favor their primal side when in wolf form. Right now, I needed Liam's brain more than his brawn. Plus, it was nice to have someone to talk to. I'd spent so much time working solo, Liam's presence was a welcome respite from my own company. I was glad Alaric suggested him.

"Just FYI, if you need me to blow up the whole island, I'm going to need more supplies."

"I don't think the island itself is the problem." It might simply be housing the problem.

We scampered to the top of a pile of rocks and stopped at the sight of a giant on the other side. Its large body was covered in identical oval markings.

"Somebody's a big fan of tattoos," Liam whispered.

My breathing hitched. "Those aren't tattoos."

"I'd like to say they're hideously large freckles left over from before the Eternal Night." Liam's swallow was audible. "But they're not, are they?"

I shook my head. "They're eyes."

Liam ducked his head. "Terrific. We travel all this way only to contend with the Eyes of March."

I shot him a quizzical look. "You mean the Ides of March."

"No, I mean Eyes." He gestured to his own set. "What is it?"

"If I had to guess, I'd say it's an argus."

"Argus? Like that Greek monster with a hundred eyes?"

"Just like that, except argus is a species, not an individual."

"Good to know. How do we kill it?"

"I don't know that killing it is the right call. I want to

know what it's doing here." And how did it get here in the first place?

"Oh, great. What's your plan? Request an interview? I'm sure he'll be amenable. He seems plenty social all the way out here by himself."

At least he wasn't a heart-eater. I frowned. Why wasn't he a heart-eater and why were there none here? No sign of keeluts either.

"What's wrong?" Liam whispered. "Having second thoughts?"

"No. Just having too many thoughts. Are you picking up any other scents?"

Liam sniffed the air around us. "A couple, but they're faint. Whatever was here isn't here anymore. The strongest one is right in front of us."

All at once the eyes popped open, revealing burning blue irises. Even worse, every single one seemed trained on us.

Fear seized hold of me.

Liam's voice rang out. "Move!"

I ducked as a tree branch-sized arm whooshed over my head.

I twisted to glare at the werewolf. "Move? That was your contribution? What if I moved the wrong way?"

Liam shrugged. "I panicked."

The giant lumbered toward us, smashing rocks along the way. The hill of rocks shifted, and I grabbed Liam's arm as he lost his balance. Together we scurried to the left side of the pile before we ended up buried in rubble.

Dozens of eyes tracked our movements. There'd be no sneaking past him. We'd have to find another way.

"I don't think I'll be putting this guy to sleep with a chokehold," Liam said. "Can you use his blood?"

With eerie blue eyes that matched the two bloodless monsters, I had the sinking feeling the answer was no. "I'll do my best."

"I can't even distract him for you," Liam complained. "He can watch us both at the same time." His brow furrowed. "By the gods, he'd make an excellent babysitter. Do you think we could persuade him to move to the Wasteland with all those kids?"

"First we have to persuade him not to kill us."

"Good point."

I tried to form a connection with the giant and was surprised to feel the flow of blood. As tendrils of magic mingled with the giant's blood, the argus swiped Liam off the rock and started to squeeze.

I *pushed* my magic through the giant's bloodstream and willed it to slow.

"Hurry," Liam choked out.

"You can't rush genius," I called back. I was hoping the joke would ease his fears, but I fully recognized it was hard to laugh when a giant was squeezing your lungs.

Dozens of eyes watched me to see if I would intervene. The giant didn't seem to sense the presence of magic. In fairness, it took a lot more effort on my part to influence his system. A giant the size of an argus meant more blood I had to control.

The giant began to sway to the side, still clutching Liam in his grip. If he crashed into the rocks, Liam might end up dead anyway.

Multiple sets of eyes fluttered and closed. His large hand relaxed and Liam slipped to the ground.

"Run!" I yelled.

Liam bolted as the giant tipped to the side and collapsed. The huge body landed amidst the hill of rocks and sent them flying in all directions. One rock skimmed the top of my head as it sailed past.

Panting, Liam stood with his head between his knees for a moment.

"Are you okay?" I asked.

His head bobbed up and down.

"He had blood."

Liam stood upright. "So I gathered."

I surveyed the area. The hill was now gone and the sleeping giant was sprawled across the scattered rocks.

"Lumpy pillows," Liam remarked. "He'll be sore when he wakes up."

"As long as we're not here by then, I don't care."

Beneath one of the rocks, something glinted in the darkness. I ventured forward to investigate.

"What is it?" Liam's voice cut through my intense concentration.

"I'm not sure yet." I reached for the shiny sliver and tugged. The rock toppled to the side revealing layers of metal. The top piece was a rectangular sheet, slightly curved and about two feet in length.

"Hey, look." Liam reached behind a different rock and produced a rustic helmet. "What's the history of the island? Any forts here before the Great Eruption?"

"The island wasn't even here then." Unless the records were wrong, which wasn't out of the realm of possibility. We'd have to figure it out later. Right now, we needed to gather our discovery and head back to the city.

"Maybe it belongs to the argus."

"It's ours now."

Liam observed me as I cleaned off the dirt. "How are we going to transport all this back? It'll sink the boat."

I lifted three of the pieces. "No, it won't. Feel them. They're awkward but not as heavy as they seem."

He stuffed his head into the helmet. The bottom edges swallowed the upper half of his body. "Nope. That won't work." He removed the helmet and hugged it against his chest. "You can put the rest in my backpack."

I opened the bag and shoved the pieces inside. They were so big that I was unable to zip it closed. "Let's get back to the boat before we forget where we left it."

"I was thinking before the argus wakes up, but your reason works too."

We scrambled over the rocks and followed our trail back to our starting point.

Liam scratched his head. "Um, you were joking before about forgetting where we left the boat, right?"

I scanned the area. This was definitely the place. I recognized the indentation on the largest rock. It was shaped like the letter 'c.'

In the distance a glimmer of movement caught my eye. "I see it." Unfortunately, what I saw was the dinghy floating away. I hadn't considered the tide rolling in.

Liam dropped the backpack on the sand. "Now what? I'm not much of a swimmer."

"I am." I peeled off my clothes and boots until only my underwear remained.

"You sure you want to do that?"

"I don't see another option, do you?" I waded into the water. Once the waves reached my knees, I started to swim. The current was strong, which probably explained the position of the dinghy. I focused on each stroke and tried not to think about the monsters lurking beneath the surface. Maybe they wouldn't notice a small fish like me, or maybe they avoided the island like the aptu.

A lightning strike encouraged me to move faster. My teeth chattered so hard that I bit my tongue. The pain helped snap the boat into focus.

I pulled the water past me. Something tickled the bottom of my foot. I prayed it was only a fish passing too close to me. The dinghy was only a few feet away now, although the waves seemed to be pushing the vessel away from me with each stroke.

I swept my arm overhead and latched on to the edge. Once I had a proper grip on it, I pulled myself close enough to climb aboard. I was relieved to see the oars still in place. We'd be at a complete loss without them.

I waved to Liam and rowed to shore. He didn't wait for me to get close enough. He bounded through the surf and launched himself into the dinghy, along with the backpack and helmet. The boat rocked and I quickly steadied it to keep it from capsizing.

"I'll take the first shift," he offered.

I didn't argue. I was pretty drained from the swim. I settled against the side of the boat and tried to rest.

"You could be anywhere else right now, you know," he said, once we were out in the open water again. "Britannia City. Minneapolis. The Southern Territories. Yet here you are, risking life and limb for a city that enslaved you."

I didn't bother to open my eyes. "Your point?"

"You must really love him. That's my point."

Ignoring the remark, I turned to the side and tried to get comfortable.

"The wind's in our favor," Liam said.

Small mercies.

"What I wouldn't give for an aptu right now," Liam said. "A statement I never thought I'd make."

We switched halfway back to the city. I was still tired

and sore, but a deal was a deal. If I ever expected Liam to accompany me on another suicide mission, I had to do my part.

As the waves grew higher, Liam burst into song. I couldn't decide whether he was trying to distract me or himself. He warbled through *New York, New York*, a classic pre-Eternal Night song.

"I was supposed to leave today," I grumbled.

"You've been singing that same tune every day. I'm not buying it. Besides, the singer's going to the city, not leaving it," Liam pointed out.

"Whatever."

I was fairly certain I'd dislocated my shoulder some-where between the swim to the boat and now. The throb-bing intensified and I started to sweat from the pain.

"You okay, Britt?"

"Fine," I ground out. I wasn't going to admit defeat. I had an ego to uphold, after all.

As we approached the Statue of Liberty, I noticed a dragon perched on the torch. It breathed fire as we passed, which made the torch look aglow.

The dragon's gaze tracked us.

"We have a tail," Liam remarked.

I turned to see the dragon gliding behind us. It probably wanted to piggyback into the city. Dragons were desperate to infiltrate places where they were banned.

Liam waved.

"What are you doing?" I hissed.

"Trying to be friendly. I don't want it to attack us before we get to safety."

"Don't wave to dragons. It looks aggressive."

Sure enough, the dragon unleashed a torrent of fire.

The flames streaked over our heads and disintegrated when they hit land, activating the city ward.

"Thank the gods for that," I murmured.

Liam's hand dropped to his side. "Fine. No more Mr. Nice Guy." He cast a wary glance at me. "Any chance you can row faster? The dragon looks pretty pissed."

"Not with only one good arm."

"Come on! I only waved at you!" He dropped to the seat. "You'd think I stole a baby from the nest the way it's acting."

My muscles screamed in protest as I rowed harder and faster.

Liam's voice rang out. "We're going to crash!"

There was no time to swerve. The dinghy slammed into the dock and sent us flying. I ignored the bumps and bruises I was sure to have. We were on land. We were safe. The dragon had returned to its perch.

Grinning from ear to ear, Liam waved again. "Better luck next time, sucker!"

I yanked his hand down. "Very mature."

He turned his grin to me. "Make sure that's the inscription on my tombstone, would you?"

Chapter Nine

L iam and I delivered our findings to the compound, where Alaric was thoughtful enough to have a hot meal and a pitcher of beer waiting for us in the dining hall.

"You really know the way to a werewolf's heart," Liam remarked as he polished off his second beer.

Alaric's mouth twitched with amusement. "Now that your heart and stomach are content, are you ready to tell me what you found?"

Liam burped and clamped a hand over his mouth. "I beg your pardon, Your Majesty."

"No keeluts or heart-eaters," I said, "but there was an argus."

Alaric refilled my glass, gallant vampire king that he was. "An actual argus?"

I nodded. "His eyes were the same blue as the other two monsters."

"What does that mean? They're all from the same creepy family?" Liam asked.

"I think it means they're all connected somehow." Except, of course, the argus had blood.

"Traditionally an argus was a guardian," Alaric said, more to himself.

Liam dragged his sleeve across his mouth. "Like a dragon guarding treasure?"

I shook my head. "A dragon protects his own possessions. An argus protects for someone else."

But who?

"Then what was he guarding on the island? The only thing we found was the pile of junk we brought back."

"Junk," I repeated. Like the breastplate. "Let's take a closer look at those scraps."

We emptied the contents of our bags on the table and spread the metal fragments across the surface for a better view.

"I love puzzles," Liam declared. "Remember that one we did of the basket of kittens?"

"You mean the one you did. I watched and drank all your cheap beer out of boredom."

Liam looked stricken. "But kittens."

I studied the pieces. "Lots of rectangles."

"Those match," Liam said. He pointed to two of the fragments. "And those two."

I pulled them closer to us and set them next to each other. "You're right." One pair was longer than the other.

"Looks like a shin guard," Liam said. "I used to wear them for soccer."

"You wore metal shin guards? Must've been hard to run in those."

Liam ripped the item from my hand and placed it against his shin. "Okay, so maybe it's for someone a little taller and wider than me. If these belong to the argus, then why wasn't he wearing them?"

"I don't think they belong to him. I think this might be the treasure he was guarding."

"He and I have different definitions of treasure," Liam said.

Alaric joined me as I examined the remaining pieces.

"Same substance as the breastplate," he murmured.

I repositioned the fragments. "Because they're from the same suit of armor."

Alaric's eyebrows inched up. "Let's be sure." The king turned to a member of staff lingering by the doorway. "Fetch Olis and tell him to bring the breastplate."

I folded my arms. "I don't get it. If these were on the island with a protector, why was the breastplate buried in a tunnel beneath the city?"

Liam glanced at the fragments. "Maybe someone found it on the island years ago and brought it back here."

"And the argus let them take the breastplate? I don't think so."

"Why would an argus be protecting a suit of armor in the first place?" Alaric mused.

"And on Hudson Island of all places." I sighed. "I think we need to know more about this suit."

Liam pointed to the helmet. "Whoever it's for, he's a big guy."

"And powerful enough to command an argus," Alaric added.

I snapped my fingers. "Heart-eaters can only be created by a god or goddess."

Liam paled. "Somehow that information doesn't give me the warm fuzzies."

"Which deity sent the beast here and why?" Alaric asked.

"If only the internet were still a thing," Liam said with a regretful sigh.

Although I was vaguely familiar with the concept of the internet, I didn't know much about it other than humans relied on it for information before the Great Eruption. Once the supervolcanoes blew their stacks, the deracinated earth and dysfunctional satellites rendered the internet unusable. The powers-that-be tried to use magic to power it, but technology turned out to be harder to control than nature, and so the internet passed into history. To the delight of librarians and academics, books once again took pride of place as the primary source of information.

"Your Majesty, you requested the breastplate." Olis appeared in the dining hall carrying the fragment.

"On the table, please," Alaric said.

Olis set the piece at the end of the table, unaware of our puzzle.

"Let me do the honors." Liam reached across the table for the breastplate and inadvertently knocked over a candelabra in the process. "Shit. That's what you get for compensating me with beer."

Before we could stop it, the fire reached the breastplate and set it alight.

"The armor!" I yelled.

Alaric ripped a tapestry from the wall and smothered the flames. We all stared in awe.

Although the wood at the end of the table was charred, the breastplate was unaffected.

Alaric touched the piece of metal with his index finger. "It isn't even warm. What kind of armor is impervious to fire?"

"One that's enchanted," Olis said.

Alaric examined the unblemished fragment. "No, it's more than that. There's something about this metal. It isn't regular armor."

"That's because it's ancient and five times your size," Liam said.

Ancient. I had a feeling this type of metal was not only old but also out of circulation or we'd have seen a lot more of it by now.

Liam poured another glass of beer, oblivious to the judgmental look of the wizard. "Cool. Now what?"

I swiped the breastplate from the table. "I know a guy."

"I think you'll find *we* know a guy," Olis corrected me.

"I know, but he likes me better."

"Who doesn't?" Liam quipped.

Olis pushed the pitcher of beer out of the werewolf's reach.

"Keep the other pieces in a safe place," I advised. "I'd suggest a cloaking spell, too. You don't want monsters popping up inside the compound in search of them."

"Or an argus," Liam said.

"The argus isn't a warrior," I countered. "He'll either stay on the island or go back to wherever he came from."

"Or be executed for his failure," Alaric added.

"Okay, *now* I feel bad." Liam slumped against the back of the chair.

Olis pivoted to me. "Would you like me to accompany you when you take the metal for examination? Our friend might be more willing to help when there's an official request."

"I'll be fine. He doesn't know I'm no longer a servant of House August. Anyway, I'd rather keep this quiet. If I show up with the Director of Security, tongues will be wagging."

Liam's eyelids began to close. "As a werewolf, I object to that phrasing."

Alaric turned to a member of staff. "Someone see that our inebriated guest makes it home safely."

I mouthed *thank you*.

Lee Mahoney worked out of an old Duane Reade on the corner of 8th and 41st Streets. If you squinted, you could still see the faint letters of the drugstore's name above the entrance. Lee was a popular blacksmith with a royal contract, which was how we became acquainted. He crafted a few of the weapons I acquired as a member of the House August security team. Technically I should hand those weapons over to Olis now that I was a free witch, but as nobody had demanded their return, I considered them part of my severance package.

Lee was busy with a customer when I entered the smithy. We made eye contact and he held up a finger. I forced myself to exercise patience and took the opportunity to admire some of Lee's handiwork on display. The smithy wasn't the usual hovel that reeked of coal dust and iron. My nostrils didn't burn here.

As evidenced by the impressive display, Lee took great pride in his work. He treated it equal parts art to be admired and utilitarian item with a function, which was probably one of the reasons House August awarded him with such a prestigious contract.

I felt something rub against my leg and looked down to see Cleo. The resident cat met my gaze and meowed. I crouched down to honor her request. Arguably it was more of a demand, but I was happy to oblige. Once upon a time cats would've been coveted pets to keep the mice and rats at bay. Now that rats were the size of feral hogs, however, cats outgrew their usefulness and people couldn't afford another mouth to feed. Not only that but the former predators were now the prey. Not a great position for cats to find themselves in.

"What does the wizard need now?" Lee asked once the customer departed. "I only fulfilled his order last week. You'd think we were under siege."

"I'm not here for Olis." I bumped a hip against the counter. "I have a question for you."

"You personally? Or you on behalf of House August?"

"Do you care?" As I guessed, he hadn't heard the news about me. Not that it mattered. Even though I no longer had an official role, I was still here on an errand for the king.

"Guess not." His gaze slid to the bag looped over my shoulder. "You got a present for me?"

I set the bag on the counter between us. "I'll need you to lock the door before I show you what's in here."

Lee whistled. "Now you've got my attention." He hurried from behind the counter and locked the door. "Is it a robot?"

"Don't think so."

"Too bad. Robots are pretty cool."

"When have you ever seen a robot?"

"My friend Krupke has one of those old grocery store robots that would roll around the floor and offer help to shoppers. He keeps it in his apartment as a butler."

"Does it work?" I tried to picture a robot in my shoebox-sized apartment. I'd probably end up chucking it out the window after a day.

"It works well enough. He's the tinkerer I've told you about."

"Right. I remember." Krupke specialized in scavenging

old parts and creating something useful with them. I hadn't ever needed his services, but his skills were in demand by a certain population in the city. Not vampires or magic users generally. They tended to be shifters or humans with enough spare cash to spend on a bespoke machine.

Lee reached for the bag and I slapped his hand away. "Now I really want to see what's inside the bag. If you let a cat out of there, I'm going to be very disappointed."

I smiled. "Definitely not a cat."

He angled his head toward Cleo, who was now perched on one of the shelves. "That's how I found her, you know. Stuffed in a bag and left for dead."

"Well, she's thriving here. That much is obvious."

Cleo seemed to sense she was the topic of conversation and meowed.

"What I'm about to show you is highly confidential. You'd lose your contract if anyone in House August discovers that you shared this."

Lee kept his gaze riveted on the bag. "Go on then. Dazzle me."

I emptied the contents onto the counter and stopped just short of saying, "Ta-da!"

He studied the breastplate without touching it. "What is it?"

"I was hoping you could tell me."

"Looks like an oversized breastplate for a suit of armor. Maybe customized for a giant or a large troll."

"I'm more interested in the substance used to make the armor."

Lee reached for the breastplate. "May I?"

I nodded. "Stick it in the forge. It won't burn."

He arched a bushy eyebrow. "That so?"

"It was an accidental experiment."

Lee pinched the edge between his fingers and lifted it to the nearest light. "Hmm."

"Can you elaborate on that noncommittal sound?"

"Not really. I've never seen anything like it."

"Really? You're an expert in metals."

He returned the breastplate to the counter. "Not this metal. Sorry, you'll need to check with someone else."

Not this metal? How many different types of metal were there? "What kind of expert should I be looking for? A scientist? A metallurgist?"

He grunted. "Doubtful. I'd go for a historian. I'm not talking Gettysburg and World War II. I mean somebody with knowledge of the arcane. My skills are limited by my experience, which doesn't include anything like this. I wish it did, though. Metal like that would be a valuable asset for a House."

I stymied the rising disappointment. I thought for sure Lee would be able to help. "Can you recommend anyone with that kind of knowledge?"

He drummed his stubby fingers on the countertop. "I can think of someone, but you might not want to make the trek."

"Where would I have to go?"

"To Kearny."

I cringed at the thought of New Jersey. "Who's there?"

"A wise woman. She's not a professor or anything, but she knows more history than anybody I ever met, and that includes the House librarians."

"How did you meet her?"

"I lost my shirt to her in a poker game. Not a metaphor. I mean my actual shirt. Her name's Pamela."

"Last name?"

Lee shrugged. "No clue. I don't even think anybody

calls her Pamela. If you go through the Holland, ask for the wise woman. They'll know."

"Only one wise woman? There goes the neighborhood." I placed the breastplate carefully in the bag. "Thanks for your help."

"Let me know when you find out what it is. You've piqued my curiosity."

"I will." I slung the handle of the bag over my shoulder. "Take care, Lee."

I wouldn't see him again, although he didn't know that. I paused to give Cleo another head rub before I left. George would hate that I smelled like a cat, but Cleo deserved a little love and affection. We all did.

Chapter Ten

I returned to the apartment for supplies. If I was heading through the Holland Tunnel, I wasn't going unprepared. Before the Great Eruption, the tunnel was a popular thoroughfare for commuters driving between New York and New Jersey. Vehicles were no longer permitted in the tunnel, however, because it was vulnerable to tremors and thus deemed unsafe. Although House August posted guards at both ends of the tunnel, they tended to look the other way when smugglers and other small-time crooks passed through. I'd once mentioned this to Alaric, but the prince was more concerned with his personal affairs at the time and took no notice. Olis chose to turn a blind eye as well. Now that I knew about his affiliation with the Trinity Group, his disinterest made more sense.

"You ready, George?"

The phoenix burped his assent in the form of a puff of smoke.

I took a bicycle from the corner rack and rode down Sixth Avenue. The free bicycles were part of a scheme to encourage vampires to pedal around the city. Because vehicles and gasoline were coveted items, there was a tendency among wealthier vampires to flaunt their status by traveling five blocks in a car. That created a domino effect whereby even less fortunate vampires wanted to drive everywhere, no matter how short the journey. A few years ago, House August attempted to combat the trend by introducing free bicycles throughout the city. There was even a marketing campaign that featured a shirtless Alaric on a bicycle, his bare chest glistening with a sheen of perspiration. I'd torn one of the posters off a wall as a keepsake—and later to defile with a mustache and horns. In the end, the poster proved more popular than the scheme itself, but the upside was there was an ample number of bicycles available throughout the city.

I hadn't been on a bicycle since the long ride from Virginia to the Wasteland when Alaric and I had separated for the sake of our child companions. It felt good to use those muscles again.

Sixth Avenue was busier than I anticipated, so I veered off the main road and zigzagged the rest of the way to the Holland Tunnel. It was impressive that the tunnel had managed to withstand a variety of monster attacks over the years. The ward was designed to be weaker here because vampires wanted to freely travel between states. A stronger ward would've required more infrastructure and more bureaucracy, two things House August avoided.

I abandoned the bicycle a block from the tunnel. I preferred to get the lay of the land on foot. George hovered above me, awaiting instructions. There was a chance I'd need his firepower in the tunnel. Not every battle could be fought with blood, as recent engagements had taught me.

There were two vampires stationed outside the tunnel

entrance. I recognized the one on the right. His name was Dominic and he kept a gecko in his apartment, which annoyed his neighbors to no end because the gecko had a tendency to escape and show up in unexpected places—like the toilet of the next-door apartment. I was privy to all these details thanks to Bruno, a vampire on my security team who was friendly with Dominic. Between the gecko and Bruno, I figured Dominic had a high tolerance for nonsense, which made this part of the journey easier.

I strode toward them with an energetic bounce. The guards snapped to attention when they realized I was headed to the tunnel.

"Stop right there. What's your business here?" Dominic demanded.

"I need to go through the tunnel. It's the quickest route and I'm in a hurry." Which was true.

The other vampire looked me up and down. "Trust me. You don't want to go this way, honey. There are safer passages for girls like you."

"I'm going to visit my dying aunt in Kearny and this is the fastest route. If I go another way, I might not make it in time."

"You got somebody picking you up in Jersey City?" Dominic asked. "Because it's a haul to Kearny without transportation."

I gestured toward the alley behind me. "I've got a bike."

He squinted. "Wait. Don't I know you?"

"Britt," I said.

His head bobbed. "I'm Dominic, Bruno's friend."

I feigned shock and delight. "That's right." I smacked my forehead. "I thought you looked familiar. Olis gave me a day pass to visit my aunt. You can contact him to confirm if you want." I knew they wouldn't bother, but if they did, I had no doubt Olis would back my story.

Dominic glanced at his companion. "She's okay."

The second vampire didn't seem convinced. "If anything happens to her in there, it'll be our fault."

Dominic snorted. "If what Bruno says is true, she can handle herself."

The second vampire noticed George above me. "Is he traveling with you?"

"Yes. He's my emotional support phoenix. I've been upset about my aunt, so it seemed like a good idea to bring him with me."

The second vampire rolled his eyes. "I can just imagine what the boss would say if I requested an emotional support animal."

"I don't know," Dominic said. "My gecko always makes me feel better when I'm in a bad mood."

I bit back a smile.

"You're a vampire," the second guard said. "What could possibly put you in a bad mood?"

"That's offensive," Dominic shot back. "You think I can't have feelings because I have fangs? That kind of toxic attitude is why people hate us."

"No, people hate us because we use them as food."

I held up a hand. "Guys, listen. I'm pressed for time. If I'm cleared to enter, I'll just grab my bike."

"You go ahead," Dominic said without waiting for his companion to weigh in. "I hope your aunt gets better."

"Thanks." I hurried to retrieve the bicycle before the second guard objected.

When I returned, the second guard held up a hand. "Just you. No monsters in the tunnel."

"George isn't a monster."

146

"He's a rare creature thought to be extinct. That qualifies as a monster in my book."

It seemed everybody had a different definition of a monster in this city.

I tipped back my head. "I'll meet you back at the apartment, buddy. Don't worry. I'll be fine."

The guards parted to allow me passage.

"Good luck," Dominic said.

"Don't say we didn't warn you," the second vampire added.

I patted his shoulder. "Consider yourself absolved."

Pushing the bicycle past them, I entered the mouth of the tunnel. The temperature immediately seemed to drop several degrees. I didn't anticipate any problems this close to the mouth, not with the guards so close. If there were going to be obstacles, I figured they'd pop up about halfway through the tunnel.

I climbed on the seat and pushed off. The darkness was thick in the tunnel, which suited me fine. The stealthier we could be, the better.

I was almost at the halfway point when an unanticipated force knocked me off the bicycle. My backside hit the tunnel floor, causing pain to shoot up my spine. I scrambled to my feet and searched the blackened tunnel for my attacker. I glimpsed movement out of the corner of my eye and swiveled toward it. A long, greenish-black body slithered across the floor. At first glance I thought it was a freakishly large snake until I heard the whisper of my name. A shiver rushed through me. Although I'd heard of spirit eels, I'd never been unlucky enough to encounter one —until now.

The eel slithered closer. I cut a glance at my bicycle and tried to judge the distance. The monster had the advantage.

My primary goal was to avoid looking directly at its face. That's how they managed to lull you into a trance before they devoured your spirit. The eels thrived on the essences of other living creatures. They planted their slimy mouths on their victims and sucked, extracting the life force and leaving an empty husk behind.

I had no intention of falling victim to this one, no matter how many times it whispered my name like a promise.

I charged toward the bicycle. The eel's tail whipped toward me in an attempt to block me. The tail was likely the cause of my fall in the first place. I leaped over the swinging appendage and grabbed the bike's handlebars. The eel struck my back and I pitched forward, flipping over the handlebars. My spine smacked against the tire. The eel curled around the front of the bicycle and I sprang to my feet, making sure to avoid eye contact.

There was no way I could outrun a spirit eel. I needed that bicycle unless I used my blood magic. The problem with spirit eels was they could easily turn the tables on me. My efforts to control its blood could result in the eel controlling me.

"Britt," the eel whispered. The sound caressed my skin, enticing me to turn around and face the source.

Nope. Not gonna happen.

Keeping my back to the eel, I reached backward for the tire and pulled the bike. One of my muscles started to cramp thanks to the awkward angle and I groaned as I yanked the weight of the bicycle toward me.

I pushed the bike upright and climbed onto the seat. Metal scraped the bare skin of my ankle as my feet fumbled to find the pedals.

The eel struck again. This time it tried to entangle its body with the tire to stop the bike from moving.

"Britt," it said again.

My body felt compelled to turn toward the sound. I fought the urge.

The eel rose up to meet my gaze. I wrenched my face away and abandoned the bicycle. I'd have to exit the tunnel on foot with my eyes closed. Not ideal. You'd think it would be easy because of living without sunlight—that somehow my other senses would improve to compensate for the lack of visibility. That didn't seem to be the case with me, especially when I was running for my life.

I stepped on something—many somethings—as I ran toward the exit. I tried not to think about what they were. Body parts came to mind, but I shoved the thoughts aside. My focus right now was escaping the spirit eel. My spirit had better things to do than fuel the existence of a pointless monster.

I chanced a glance over my shoulder to see if I'd put distance between us. Big mistake. The spirit eel was nipping at my heels and clever enough to keep quiet about it. The monster seemed to know I'd closed my eyes and was trying to lull me into a false sense of security by falling silent. The moment it saw my face, it started its siren song all over again.

I forced myself forward, but my legs grew heavier. They were desperate to betray me, to stay right here in the tunnel, planted like trees for the eel to embrace.

"No, no, no," I muttered. I didn't battle a thousand monsters and vampires in order to die like this.

I clenched my teeth and pushed forward. Although there was no light at the end of the tunnel, I knew the exit was there. I saw a flash of movement and hoped it wasn't a second eel. They tended to be solitary creatures, but that didn't mean there was only one lurking in a tunnel the size of the Holland.

"Britt," came the coaxing sound.

Oh, gods. It suddenly felt as though I was wading through a river of chocolate. The air was thick with resistance as my body slowed. The eel shot past me and turned to claim victory. Although my mind raced with options, I couldn't seem to take action.

The eel rose up to make eye contact and I stared into two black pools of despair. It was as though I sensed every soul now trapped behind that fearsome face. I tried to force my eyelids closed but they refused to obey my mental command.

"Britt," the eel whispered.

"Yes," I replied.

A silver blade cut through the murk and sliced straight through the slender body, liberating the head from the rest. I jumped back to avoid the traces of poisonous blood that sprayed from the body. Only a small drop could kill me.

"Been trying to get this sucker for months," a voice said. "I appreciate you leading it this way."

"I can't really take credit. I was trying to escape it."

"So was my wife, Linda." His expression soured. "She didn't make it. Been hunting it every day since then, but it was smart. Knew I was there with an axe every time and went into hiding."

"Until I came along and distracted it."

He grinned. "Exactly. Much obliged, stranger."

"Same to you."

"Nah, you would've made it without my intervention." He observed me from head to toe. "What brings you through the tunnel anyway? You leaving the city?"

"I'm looking for a wise old woman."

His grin broadened. "Pamela? Why am I not surprised? I hope you brought a lucky rabbit's foot." He angled his head. "Although maybe luck's on your side today."

"Let's hope."

"Be careful, though. She's a fierce competitor," he said.

"I'm not going there to play."

"That's what my brother said. He came home without his gold teeth." His brow furrowed. "It's a bit of a hike from here."

I shrugged. "I had a bike."

He gripped the handle of the axe. "Tell you what. I've got a golf cart right over there. If you promise to leave it where you found it, I'll let you use it as a token of my appreciation for avenging my wife."

I held up a hand. "I solemnly swear to return your cart."

"Good enough for me." He used the axe to point to the cart's location. "Easy to operate. The key's already in there."

"Where'd you get your hands on a golf cart?"

"My grandad. He stored it in a warehouse that everybody thought was abandoned, along with a few other items that became more useful than people ever imagined."

"Smart man. Care to point me in the direction of Pamela's?"

"Straight to the main intersection, then a left and another left. Look for the jolly dude in the red suit and you'll find her," he advised. Resting his axe on his shoulder, he turned away and blended with the shadows. It seemed our conversation was over.

I spotted the jolly dude in the red suit in the front yard of a modest two-story house. The inflatable Santa Claus rocked back and forth in the breeze. Next to him was a partially deflated reindeer with a red nose. I knew about Christmas thanks to a couple that took me in when I was younger, the same couple that introduced me to Curious George. Although I was aware that it was a holiday tradition celebrated by humans, I'd never seen life-sized inflatables that marked the occasion. Never mind that it wasn't December.

An old woman sat on the stoop. Her short, white hair was streaked with black. She wore a floral shift dress that hit just under the knee, paired with a set of black Doc Marten boots. I'd worn a similar pair of boots when I was younger. Eventually I traded them when I realized they were heavy enough to make sneak attacks challenging. This woman didn't look like she'd be sneaking up on anything aside from an unsuspecting bottle of pain relievers.

I parked the golf cart across the street and slipped the key in my pocket.

It was only when I crossed the street that I noticed the large cat sprawled across the dirt beside the stoop. This cat was somewhere between a Cleo and a Toodles. Too large to be a regular house cat, but too small to qualify as a genuine threat.

The cat lifted its head at my approach.

"Don't make eye contact with him or he'll take it as a challenge," the old woman said.

I averted my gaze from the large cat. "What about the reindeer?"

"You can gaze into his brown eyes until the cows come home. He won't do you any harm."

"The red nose might attract unwanted attention."

Her eyes narrowed. "You selling something?"

"No. Are you Pamela?"

"Well, I sure as shit ain't the Easter Bunny." She spat on the ground. "No cards today, if that's what you're here for. Yesterday's game wore me out."

"I'm not here for poker. I'm looking for information."

She tilted her head for a better look at me. "Who sent you?"

"Nobody. I understand you're something of a history buff."

She pondered me. "Somebody in your shoes doesn't coming looking of her own accord. Who wants this information?"

Wise woman, my ass. Pamela seemed more like the Don of the history mafia. "My shoes?"

She grabbed the handrail and struggled to her feet. "You belong to them. You carry their foul smell."

"I don't belong to anyone." Not anymore.

She pressed a hand against the rail for support. "You came all the way from the city for this conversation, I take it?"

I nodded.

"Went through the tunnel, did you?"

"Yes."

She gave me a nod of approval. "All right then. Why don't we go inside where nobody can eavesdrop?" She turned to her left and yelled, "That's right, Earl! I know you're there listening, you creep." Shaking her head, she turned and marched up the steps to open the screen door. "I hope you like mead."

The front door opened into the living room. From there I could see straight through the dining room and the kitchen at the back of the house. The interior was heavily decorated. Framed photographs took the place of paint or wallpaper. There didn't seem to be any rhyme or reason to the images. They were a mishmash of people, landscapes, cityscapes, animals, and flowers.

I stared at the photo of a sunflower in a field on sunny day. "Where did you get these?"

"Depends. Some I found in trash heaps. I won that sunflower picture in a card game. Pretty, isn't it?"

I gazed at the image in wonder and tried to envision what the world looked like then, awash in color and light. It must've been beautiful beyond words.

"Can you imagine anything as bright yellow as that?" she asked.

"It would hurt my eyes to try."

Pamela crooked a finger. "Let's go, witch. I've got a nap in my future and, unless you plan to snuggle me, we need to get you out of here before then."

She entered the kitchen and pulled two pint glasses from the cabinet. "I make my own mead so no complaints about the taste."

"I wouldn't dream of insulting my host."

"Good girl." She filled the glasses with a honey-colored liquid and slid one across the counter to me. "This is what gets me out of bed in the morning."

"Everybody needs a reason." I sniffed the liquid and was surprised to discover it smelled like honey, too. Even with magic sustaining the growth of plants, honey was an extremely rare commodity thanks to the small bee population.

Pamela watched me carefully, as though reading my mind. "You'd be surprised what you can win in a card game."

"Apparently."

She raised her glass. "Salut."

I touched her glass with mine and sipped. The mead was a rare treat that I hoped to savor. "You're very talented."

She inclined her head. "When you live as long as I have,

154

you tend to develop a few skills." She sauntered to the oval table in the dining room and planted herself in a wooden chair. "Let's talk history."

As I approached the table, she pushed the leg of an adjacent chair with her boot. I sat and placed the bag on the table. "I need you to identify this metal."

Pamela peered at the bag over the rim of her glass. At the sight of the breastplate, she seemed to lose interest in the mead and set the glass on the table without drinking. "Where'd you get this?"

"It was discovered in a tunnel beneath the city."

She inched her chair forward, transfixed by the metal. "It's incredible."

"Most people seem to think it's junk."

"Most people are morons." She pulled the breastplate closer to her. "Such craftsmanship." She raised her eyes to meet mine. "Lee sent you here, didn't he?"

I nodded.

"He didn't recognize the metal," she said, more to herself. "No, I guess he wouldn't. It's from long before his time."

"But not yours?"

She cackled. "How old do you think I am?"

"I've found it best not to speculate about a woman's age."

"I've never seen the sun, but I still remember the aftershocks from the Great Eruption. Does that answer your question?"

It did. "You're not a witch, though."

She swilled the mead. "My mother was a witch, so I've got good instincts for your kind. My father was human. I didn't inherit any magic, unless you count longevity and an aptitude for gambling."

"I think many people would. Why do you know so much about history?"

"My father used to say that those who fail to learn history are doomed to repeat it."

"And?"

She remained fixated on the breastplate. "And I decided to learn enough to break the cycle. I believed the world was in dire straits because nobody bothered to learn the lessons that history tried to teach us." She shrugged. "I was nine. I foolishly thought I could make a difference."

"At least you were intent on making a positive difference."

"I don't think any child sets out to do otherwise." Her thumb stroked the metal. "I guess you already know it's enchanted."

"Is that what makes it special?"

"No, the fact that it's Damascus steel is what makes it special."

I hadn't heard of Damascus steel. "What's that?"

Her eyebrows lifted. "Doesn't ring any bells?"

"My official weapons training has been limited to what I picked up on the road as a kid."

She gave me an appraising look before returning her focus to the breastplate. "It's an ancient metal, long believed to be rooted in legend."

"But you believe it's real?"

She nodded. "Most legends are rooted in fact. I don't see why this should be an exception. So much of the ancient world was buried by ash and lava. I think we've only scratched the surface of what was lost to civilization."

"What makes you so certain this is an ancient metal? It might only look ancient because it was buried for so long."

"Lee's the best in the city, right? So skilled that he has a contract with House August, and even he couldn't identify this substance because it predates him. He's never seen a material like this one, let alone worked with it." She took another sip of mead. "He wouldn't know how to work with Damascus steel if he did have it. It's impervious to fire."

"We figured that one out by accident." The metal fragments were made from Damascus steel *and* enchanted. It seemed their creator really wanted to make certain the armor survived—but why?

Pamela finished the mead and held the breastplate against her chest. "Sadly, I don't think it's my size."

"Thankfully this isn't a Cinderella scenario." I pictured myself traveling throughout the land on behalf of the king, trying to find the true owner of the enormous breastplate.

Pamela grunted with amusement. "Why do you work for them?"

"By 'them,' I assume you mean vampires."

"Who else?"

"I started out killing them as a private contractor. Then I became an indentured servant of House August."

She looked at me. "And now?"

"Don't know yet. I'll figure it out as soon as..." I couldn't divulge too much. "As soon as I finish this last assignment for the king."

"An assignment that involves a piece of armor made from an ancient metal."

"In a nutshell. The king is a collector who likes to know more about what he's collected."

"Something he and I have in common then." She grimaced. "Don't like to think I have anything in common with a vampire."

"You probably have more in common than you think."

"I heard a rumor about a vaccine that makes human

blood taste rancid to vamps. Know anything about that, loyal servant of House August?"

"I've probably heard the same rumor you have. The king isn't in the business of sharing confidential information with his indentured servants." Pamela didn't need to know about my special relationship with Alaric. "Anyway, I appreciate your help." I started to rise from the chair.

She slapped a hand on the table, startling me. "Where do you think you're going? We haven't finished yet."

"We chatted. We drank mead. I got information."

"Yes, but we haven't played cards."

"You said you were tired from yesterday's game. Besides, I didn't come here to play cards. I came here for a history lesson."

"You got what you wanted. Now I get what I want. One game with a worthy opponent. That's all."

"I'm short on time and I don't have a lot of experience playing cards…"

"Ever play a game called Go Fish?" she interrupted. "That's an easy one. No experience required." It seemed Pamela was making an offer I couldn't refuse. She really was a Don.

"Never heard of it."

She produced a deck of cards from the pocket of her dress and slid them from the tattered cardboard box. "If I win, I get to keep the breastplate. If you win, you get to keep anything from this house you choose."

I laughed. "I can't make that bet. The breastplate isn't mine to wager."

Her face hardened. "I'm not asking, witch."

I leaned back against the chair, wanting to choose my words and tone carefully. This was a woman with a very large cat parked outside, after all.

"I told you I used to kill vampires. Want to know how?"

"I'm not afraid of you."

"Maybe old age has softened that head of yours because you should be."

The old woman cracked a smile. "I can see how you've survived such a dangerous life." She gestured to the glass in front of me. "Are you planning to finish that? If not, I'll take it. I don't like to waste any."

I slid the glass across the table to her. As delicious as it tasted, I'd had enough. I needed my wits about me if I expected to get back to the city in one piece.

Pamela shuffled the cards and dealt seven to me and seven to her.

"I can't wager the breastplate," I insisted.

"The only way to leave this house without playing is to kill me."

I sighed. "Come on, Pamela. Do we have to?"

"I have a reputation to uphold."

"Your reputation as a wise woman is intact."

"That isn't the reputation I mean."

"I'm more than happy to tell anybody who'll listen that I lost the game and forked over an expensive weapon. I'll shout it from the rooftops."

Her mouth formed a straight line. "It would be a shame to leave this world, but it's been a good run. No complaints."

I tipped my head back and groaned. "Do you have to be so stubborn?"

"I didn't survive this long by being flighty."

I lifted the cards from the table and held them close to my chest. For all I knew, Pamela was a serial cheater who'd positioned secret mirrors on the wall. "Tell me how to play and no cheating. If you cheat, I'll kill you. I won't enjoy it, but I'll do it."

"I believe you." She explained the rules of the game, which seemed simple enough. "Repeat them back so I know you understand."

"I have to be holding the card I ask for. If you ask me for a card and I have it, I can't lie. I have to give it to you." I rambled off the other rules.

"Very good. Now, do you have any Jacks?"

My stomach clenched as we started to play. There was no way I could leave the breastplate behind, but I really didn't want to kill Pamela. Why was life mainly a series of difficult choices? My best option was to win. I was competitive and a quick study, so at least I had those two things in my favor. Liam once accused me of cheating after he taught me to play darts and I proceeded to win every game that night. After that he refused to play with me again. Bless him, the werewolf was a sore loser.

Every time Pamela set her matches on the table, a wave of nausea rolled over me. I quickly calculated my odds of winning.

They weren't good.

"Go fish," Pamela instructed.

I picked the top card off the pile and felt a rush of excitement. "I fished my wish!" I waved the card at her.

"So I see. You get another turn, don't forget."

And that one stroke of luck turned the tide in my favor. Suddenly I was the one setting matches on the table until the game was over.

"You win," Pamela declared, not sounding the least bit sorry.

I stared at the cards on the table in disbelief. "Are you sure?"

She smiled. "I wouldn't lie about a thing like that. In case you haven't noticed, I like to win."

So did I.

"Take anything you'd like. The choice is yours."

My eyebrows inched up. "Anything? I thought you were exaggerating."

Her arm swept the room. "I stick to my rules. There's a nice bottle of rum in the liquor cabinet, if you're so inclined. Expensive stuff."

"What about the cat?"

She stiffened. "I guess it's only fair. That's how Zephyr came to live with me in the first place."

I choked back laughter. "You won the cat in a card game?"

"Technically it was roulette. Fair warning, though, Zephyr's a big eater."

"I'm not taking the cat," I said. "I was just testing your limits."

Relief shone in her eyes. "I have wine. It's not the best vintage, but guests seem to enjoy it."

"No, thank you." I knew what I wanted.

I walked to the living room where I removed the framed sunflower picture from the wall and slid it into the bag with the breastplate.

"I'll be sorry to part with it, but a deal's a deal. Where will you hang it?"

"Nowhere for now. I'll be leaving the city soon."

"Well, enjoy looking at it. I know I have."

As I left the house, the big cat didn't bother to raise his chin from where it rested on one large paw.

"Come back anytime," Pamela called after me. "I love a good rematch."

Chapter Eleven

By the time I returned to the compound, I was exhausted. Alaric seemed to anticipate my condition because he had a warm bath and a bottle of red wine ready for me in the royal suite.

"Is your plan to spoil me so much that I decide to stay?"

"And here I thought I was being subtle."

"Not subtle enough. I noticed a few raised eyebrows on my way into your room."

He wrapped his arms around my waist. "Do you think I care what they think?"

"No, but you should. You don't want an angry mob demanding you give up your crown."

He nuzzled my neck. "Do you truly believe that can happen because of you?"

I splayed my hands on his chest. "Yes."

"You give yourself too much power."

Hard pounding on the door caused me to jump out of his arms.

"What is it?" he barked.

The doors burst open and three vampires rushed into

the room. "There be dragons!" Timothy, the middle guard, said. Vampires were always pale, but I'd never seen one look quite so ashen.

Confusion marked Alaric's features. "Dragons? Where?"

"More importantly, how?" I asked.

"One landed on the Empire State Building," Timothy said. "Blew fire like it was claiming its territory."

Terrific. Because we didn't have enough to deal with. "How many?"

"We saw two," Timothy said.

Alaric listened with a hardened expression. "I need Olis."

"We'll fetch him, Your Majesty." Timothy bowed and the vampires retreated from the room at a hurried pace.

Alaric and I stared at each other. "Coincidence?" the king asked.

"Not sure," I replied.

The vampire looked past me to Olis, who now stood in the doorway in place of the guards.

"I was already on my way to report another hole in the ward," the wizard said.

"Any sign of our heart-eater friends?" I asked. *Or our Trinity Group friends*, I wanted to add but remained silent on the subject.

Olis shook his head. "Our intel says only dragons."

"We need two teams," Alaric commanded. "One to repair the ward and one to handle the dragons."

"Calinda has already sent out the repair team," the wizard said. "But they're holding off until I send word on how you'd like to deal with them."

Alaric frowned. "What do you mean? We can't have dragons flying around the city."

"Then we have your permission to kill them, Your Majesty?"

"Of course," he said.

A small gasp escaped me. I couldn't help but think of George. Even though I knew he was a phoenix, that didn't change the fact that, for years, I believed him to be a small dragon.

"What about an extraction?" I proposed.

Alaric snorted. "Dragons are a bit bigger than the average extraction target."

"Let me try something first."

Alaric peered at me. "Try what? Inviting them for tea and cake?"

"Remember the Wasteland," I said.

He nodded. "Hard to forget."

"Remember what I did in the White House."

His expression clouded over. "Also hard to forget."

During a fight in the White House with a Frankenmonster, I discovered I could control multiple bloodlines at once. I'd recently managed it with two vampires in the alley. There was no reason to believe I couldn't apply that ability to two dragons as well.

"Let me try to guide them out. They might be shooting fire because they're scared, not because they want to raze the city."

Alaric offered a crisp nod. "Tell the repair team to stand down until they're given a green light."

Olis inclined his head. "You'd like to give the dragons a chance to leave first, Your Majesty? Is that wise? The damage they could do in a matter of minutes..."

"I'm giving Britt the chance to send them out, then you can close the ward. If the plan fails or takes long enough to cause harm to the city, you have my permission to execute them. Public safety first."

Dragons had a mixed reputation. They were capable of mass destruction, yet they were still beautiful, majestic creatures that protected their families and longed to find a proper place in the world.

I understood them.

The intensity of Alaric's gaze pierced my heart. "Be careful, Britt. It's one thing to lose you of your own accord. It's quite another to lose you to death. One of those is permanent."

I placed a reassuring hand on his shoulder. "You can't lose what you never had."

"Such cheek." Smiling, he grabbed my hand and brought it to his lips. The sensation sent tiny jolts of pleasure through me.

I withdrew my hand. "I'll report back when it's done."

"That's what Olis is for. You come back to me in one piece. That's your job."

I saluted him. "Throw in a three-course meal and consider it done." I turned and followed Olis from the room. "Do we know which type of dragon?"

"No, the patrol team is unfamiliar with dragon breeds."

"That's the downside of keeping them out of the city so effectively."

Olis made an amused noise at the back of his throat. "Do you really think you can wrangle them with your magic?"

"I don't know, but it's worth a try."

"You've killed many times before. Why not kill dragons?"

"It's not that I'm opposed on principle, but maybe they wandered through the ward by accident and now they feel trapped and are lashing out. If I can guide them back through the hole and then you reseal it, isn't that a better outcome for both parties?"

"Indeed." He continued to look at me for a beat too long.

"What is it?" I prompted.

"Nothing." The wizard resumed walking. "I'm beginning to understand, that's all."

I chased after him. "Understand what?"

"You."

I snorted. "I'm glad one of us does."

It didn't take long to reach the corner of Thirty-Fourth and Fifth. The area had already been evacuated by the security team, which made my job a little easier. The fewer distractions, the better.

I tipped back my head for a decent view. One dragon was still atop the needle of the building. The second one hovered nearby, its dark green and red wings spread wide. From this distance, the dragons appeared mid-sized, about twenty feet in length. They were Devil Dragons, though, the largest species of dragon in the world. That meant these two were likely juveniles, either orphaned or separated from the herd. I felt compelled to do everything in my power to help them.

The air above me stirred and I noticed George hovering close to me. "George, I appreciate your help, but it isn't safe for you here. I need you to go."

The phoenix didn't seem to like that command. He squawked in protest and continued to hover.

"Listen, I need to concentrate and I can't do that if I'm worried about you." I pointed to the top of the building. "I'm going to try to control those two and help escort them out of the city." It was a monumental task and I wasn't certain I'd be successful, which was another reason it was safer for George to leave. If I failed, I might end up with two royally pissed-off dragons.

George seemed to acquiesce. He gave my head a gentle tap with his claws before flying in the direction of the apartment.

I returned my focus to the dragons. "Where's the hole?"

Olis pointed to a patch of black against an otherwise charcoal sky, to the left of the dragons. "It's not terribly big. They must've squeezed through."

"They probably smelled food and followed their noses." I couldn't blame them. The smell of tacos could lure me into the fiery pits of hell. "Any chance this is the work of the Trinity Group?"

I expected him to immediately object. To my surprise, he shrugged. "I wouldn't rule out the possibility. If they're responsible, though, I wasn't privy to the plan."

I'd worry about them later. "I'd like to get closer."

Olis looked at me askance. "Is that wise?"

"There's nothing wise about this, but I have a better shot if I'm closer."

"Perhaps it would be best if you keep your distance. Your safety is paramount."

I held up a hand to stop him. "Two hats, Olis, remember? Right now, you've got your security hat on."

Olis observed me for a moment. "There's a balcony on the 103rd floor." He motioned to two vampires at the building's entrance. "Good luck, Britt."

"Don't worry. If I die, I won't tell anybody you're the one to blame."

The wizard rolled his eyes. "Gods have mercy."

I sprinted to the entrance, past the two guards, and walked straight into the open elevator. "Now that's service."

I pressed the button for the observation deck and waited. The quick ride to the 103rd floor turned my stomach, and it took me a second to recover once I emerged from the elevator. I made my way to the balcony outside and was immediately struck in the face by a blast of cold air. It was several degrees cooler up here and I was feeling every degree.

I walked along the balcony to identify the targets. The second dragon was still hovering but had moved closer to its companion. That was helpful.

I rubbed my arms to keep myself warm. Any distraction ran the risk of thwarting the entire enterprise. I gazed at the dragons and tried to form a connection. Although I could feel the flow of blood, I wasn't certain that I'd tapped both dragons. They were the same species, so their blood 'felt' the same to me. I decided to continue. If I discovered I'd only connected with one, I'd handle them individually and hope the second one didn't fly off before I'd finished.

I closed my eyes and let the pulsing sensation flow through me. The connection was too loose to act on and, despite my efforts, I only seemed able to form a link with one. I needed a tighter bond. Tendrils of magic laced through the dragon's blood and I held firm. Once I was satisfied with the intensity of the bond, I attempted to steer the dragon toward the hole. It was only when I opened my eyes that I realized I'd attached myself to the hovering friend instead. It would have to do.

"Come on, buddy," I whispered. As gently as possible, I tugged the dragon toward the black patch. The resistance was swift and immediate. So powerful, in fact, that I staggered backward and lost the connection.

I shook it off and tried again. This time I was less gentle in my effort to control the dragon. My palms began to sweat as I urged it toward the hole and was relieved when its wings began to flap. Movement ensued. I *pushed*. The dragon seemed to drift aimlessly through time and space as I guided it toward the exit. Too bad there wasn't a blinking neon sign to show the dragon the way out. With a final shove, the dragon was through the ward. Of course, the job wasn't over yet. There was a chance it would re-enter in search of its friend before the repair team had a chance to work. I had to act quickly.

I changed my position on the balcony and looked at the other dragon, still perched on the needle. Timothy had said it was staking its territory, but I thought it seemed more frightened than scary. Still, a fearful dragon was every bit as dangerous, maybe even more so. I'd have to be careful.

I caught the dragon's eye and reached out to form a connection. The dragon blocked my effort and opened its maw. I spun away as a stream of fire shot toward me. Okay, I'd upset this one. Wouldn't be the first time.

I ducked behind a metal beam and made another attempt. The dragon surprised me by swooping toward me. I attempted to flee inside, but it rammed into the side of the balcony. The structure shook. I broke into a cold sweat. Heights didn't usually bother me, but over a hundred stories stretched my limits.

I reached for the door handle as the dragon made a second pass. Its massive body slammed against the balcony, and I heard the sickening sound of groaning metal. If the building toppled, I'd be dead and take the entirety of midtown with me. *Great legacy, Britt. I'm sure they'll erect a statue in your honor right beside the one of the ten super-volcanoes.*

I didn't want to hurt the dragon, but I couldn't let it destroy half the city either. My heart thrummed as I attempted to connect with the dragon's blood again. The dragon objected mightily, emitting a deafening shriek. Glass shattered and fell from the windows. My breathing hitched as the building swayed. It wasn't a large movement, but it was enough to send me into survival mode. I needed to get out of the building. If I left now, though, the dragon would continue to wreak havoc.

The dragon flew about ten feet away and turned toward me. The glint in its amber eye told me it was executing one final pass. I stood my ground and waited, a plan forming. It was a risk, albeit a calculated one. I'd spent my life calculating risk. I should be an expert by now—'should' being the critical word.

The dragon shot toward the building. I climbed on the balcony barrier and perched on the rim. The dragon swerved as it reached the balcony in order to hit the building broadside again.

I jumped.

The scales were cooler and smoother than I anticipated. Startled by my sudden move, the dragon lurched and pulled up, avoiding contact with the structure. I scrambled to the creature's neck and locked my arms as far around it as they could reach. The dragon bucked, unhappy to have been boarded without permission. Tightening my grip, I released my magic. The physical contact helped boost the connection. I felt the magic lock into place and urged the dragon in the direction of the hole. I glanced down to see where I could land once I'd steered our interloper to the exit.

Nowhere.

The hole was directly above Fifth Avenue. I turned back to the sky. The dragon was nearing the black patch. If I didn't drop off now, the dragon was exiting the city with a passenger.

A one-way ticket was not on my schedule today. I

promised Alaric I'd return to him in one piece. And I desperately wanted that three-course meal.

I could guide the dragon close enough to the ground where I could safely land, but if the connection broke, I'd have to wrangle the beast all over again, which would be much harder with me on the ground and the dragon high in the sky.

I quickly weighed my other options. They all sucked.

The dragon rode the wind like a boat cresting over the waves. There was a certain grace to the movements. I would have loved to take time to appreciate them, but I was too busy trying not to die.

Over the top of the dragon's head, the black patch sparked with green light. Oh, no. The repair team had started. No doubt they planned to seal the hole the moment the dragon passed through it. Did they know I was on its back? Unlikely. I'd be a dot on its scales, and no one had witnessed my jump from the balcony.

Once the ward was active, I'd have no choice but to ride the dragon until it landed elsewhere. Dragons could travel for a thousand miles before they stopped to rest. I could slow its blood and force it to land, but there was a risk I'd overdo it and kill us both when we crashed.

Stop the ride! I want to get off.

The dragon approached the hole, still under my control. More green light sparked along the patch. My jaw clenched. I'd have to take my chances on the dragon. The odds of survival were greater, but the inconvenience of traveling a thousand miles back to New York...Well, I'd been planning to leave anyway.

As the dragon's head passed through, a touch of magic jolted it. It reared up and knocked me backward. I slid down the smooth scales, unable to gain purchase. A scream stuck in my throat.

The dragon sailed through the hole and I continued to slide, bouncing off the backside and hitting the tail.

I fell like a starfish on its back, arms and legs spread into points. At first I felt like a leaf drifting through the air. At some point, though, gravity seized hold of me and *pulled*. I plummeted toward the earth and watched as the dragon's tail slipped through the hole just as the magic repaired the damage. The ward was intact.

And I was about to die.

My eyes seemed to close against their will as the city rushed past me from the top down. Familiar images flashed in my mind. Alaric. Liam. I was surprised to see my parents, standing beside the forest in Lancaster. I wouldn't have guessed they'd be on my mind during my final moments. They wouldn't mourn me. They wouldn't even know I died.

It took me seconds to register that my speed had slowed. I should be moving faster, not slower. My body started to float again. With my eyes still closed, I felt as though I was being cradled by the sea, drifting over gentle waves. A sense of calm washed over me. Maybe I was already dead.

I popped open one eye and saw George hovering above me. The other eye opened and I dared to glance down. My body floated above Fifth Avenue. A row of witches stood below me, their hands joined and their chanting now loud enough to hear. Their cloaks were green and gold—Alaric's colors.

My back brushed against a hard surface. They'd lowered me to the pavement. I rolled to my knees and promptly vomited. Wiping my chin with my sleeves, I spotted a familiar pair of boots in front of me. I lifted my head to meet his gaze.

"Welcome back," Olis said.

I struggled to my feet. "I assume you got approval to use magic that powerful."

A smile tugged at his thin lips. "Do you really think the king would deny it?"

"Thank you, Olis." I knew in my heart that the wizard had saved me for his own selfish purposes—for the Trinity Group—but right now I didn't care. I was happy to be alive.

I still had miles to go before I could sleep.

Chapter Twelve

A good meal, a hot bath, and a few hours of sleep and I'd be back in action—at least that's what I told myself.

I entered the compound supported by two guards. In the dining hall, Alaric took one look at me and spat his liquor into his glass. "Good gods, Britt. Are you hurt?"

"I'm perfectly fine." I waved the guards away, hoping to show the king I was capable of standing on my own two feet. Unfortunately, my body betrayed me. I swayed to the side and Alaric caught me before I dropped to the floor.

"Yes, I can see that." He slipped an arm around my waist to keep me upright.

"The ward is intact, Your Majesty," one of the guards said.

"And the dragons?"

"Gone, thanks to Britt."

I thumped the king on the chest with a weak fist. "You owe me a meal."

"Sounds like I owe you more than that."

He dismissed the guards as Toodles plodded into the

dining hall. At the sight of me, the beast sprinted toward me and threw her massive paws on my shoulders. Alaric kept a firm grip on me to stop me from plummeting to the floor.

"Nice to see you, too, Toodles." I rubbed her nose with mine and she returned her paws to the floor where they belonged.

The king's lips skimmed my cheek. "Let's get you in a warm bath."

"Good idea. You'll join me, won't you?"

"I'm not sure that's such a good idea. You look like you narrowly escaped death."

"Exactly. I don't want to pass out and drown. I need a spotter."

His mouth turned up at the corners. "I see. This is a matter of self-preservation."

"Exactly. I've been in enough life-or-death situations today." I inhaled his familiar scent. "I'm so glad you're holding me right now. I thought my body was going to end up scattered in a million pieces across New York."

Before I could warn him that I'd vomited, he kissed me. "Then I would've sent scouts throughout the city to find every piece and put you back together again."

An idea clicked into place. "Say that again."

Alaric's brow lifted. "Because it was romantic or disgusting?"

"Kissing me after I vomited is disgusting." I clutched his shirt in my fist. "Finding pieces and sending scouts to collect them. What does that remind you of?"

His green eyes blazed with understanding. "The armor."

My aches and pains gave way as ideas pushed their way through the discomfort. "What if the armor belonged to someone's beloved and they sent their scouts to collect them as an attempt to preserve their memory?"

"It would have to be a god or a goddess, wouldn't it? The Cor-Comedere can only be created and controlled by a deity."

"Good point."

"Why don't we think on our way to the bath?" Alaric guided me from the dining hall and down a long corridor to the royal suite.

"What if the armor belonged to someone dangerous or reviled? Someone so horrible that people scattered the parts to make sure their tormentor could never return?"

Alaric deposited me on the edge of the bathtub while he turned on the taps. "Why scatter the armor but not the body?"

I shrugged. "Maybe it was symbolic."

"Except the armor's enchanted," he reminded me.

"The enchantment might have nothing to do with being drawn and quartered. If the owner was a warrior, the enchantment could've been performed for protection in battle."

"If the pieces were scattered, why were six of them on the island?"

"Because those were the pieces that had already been collected," I said. "Once Scout unearthed the missing breastplate, it probably tripped a magical wire. The rest of the armor was brought close by while the monsters work to claim the final piece." This might be the breakthrough we needed to understand what was happening. "We should talk to the House librarian about deities. Identify a god or goddess so deeply in love that they'd send their minions to the ends of the earth to find the missing pieces of their beloved."

Alaric stared at me with a strange expression.

"What?"

"Interesting that you assume it must be someone deeply in love."

"Why else would someone go to such great lengths?"

"Why else, indeed?" His head dipped and he kissed me firmly on the mouth. "How about that bath now?"

"You taste like peppermint."

"Is that good or bad?"

"My stomach is still nauseated from the fall, so good."

He grinned. "Glad to be of service. Can I get you a medicinal potion while you're in the bath?"

"I'll be fine."

"You're a witch, Britt. You're not impervious to pain." He turned off the taps and faced me. "You know what I think?"

"Enlighten me, Your Majesty."

"I think deep down you believe you deserve to feel every inch of pain and suffering."

"Maybe I do."

He shook his head. "Drink the potion. Let yourself feel better. If you won't do it for yourself, then do it for me."

I glanced at the bath. "No bubbles?"

He reached for a bottle and emptied a teaspoon of pink powder into the water. A mass of bubbles exploded on the surface. "Better?"

"Much."

Once Alaric left to retrieve the pain potion, I undressed and slipped into the silky water. The bath was warm and relaxing, and the meal afterward was hot and three-course, as promised. I even indulged in an extra crescent roll with melted butter. I salivated when a plate of chocolate cake was set in front of me on a tray on the king's four-poster bed.

Rich, dark liquid pooled around the base of the moist cake and purple petals adorned the frosting.

"It's a House favorite," Alaric said. "I thought you might like it. The petals are edible."

"I haven't even tasted it yet and it's my new favorite thing." It looked almost too good to eat. "Don't you think edible flowers might be a waste of magic?"

Alaric sliced through his cake with a fork. "It isn't a waste if it brings you joy."

I chewed the purple flowers, along with the frosting. The combination of flavors was deeply satisfying. "Consider my argument withdrawn, Your Majesty." I wolfed down the cake in record time and scraped the melted chocolate from the plate. Waste not, want not.

He regarded me. "How do you feel now?"

"Like a new witch. Thank you." I patted my slightly bulging stomach. "A new witch who will be in need of new pants by tomorrow."

"That can be arranged."

I swung my legs to the side of the bed, prompting an objection from Alaric.

"Where do you think you're going?"

"The library to investigate our theory," I said.

Alaric's eyes widened. "You can't be serious, Britt. You fell two hundred feet."

"But didn't go splat." I held out my arms and shook my wrists. "See? All one piece."

He aimed his finger at me. "You will not leave this compound until tomorrow. Is that clear?"

I moved the tray to the console table against the wall. "And how do you propose to stop me?"

A sly grin emerged. "If I recall correctly, you have a fondness for restraints."

My eyes narrowed. "That doesn't sound like a restful night of sleep, Your Majesty."

"No, it doesn't," he admitted. "And I would like to give you a chance to recover. If there are more monsters to fight, I want you refreshed and ready, although selfishly I'd prefer you be refreshed and ready for me."

"Some might consider you a monster. Maybe that qualifies you."

He looked visibly stricken. "Bit harsh."

"Sorry, I shouldn't have said that. You know I don't think that." Not anymore, at least.

His expression softened. "I know. You should sleep now. I'll have the fire prepared."

"I don't have a fireplace in my room."

He motioned to the adjacent wall. "No, but I do. I'm not leaving you alone tonight, Britt. I want to be certain you're okay."

This was the Alaric I'd fallen in love with years ago. The one I'd convinced myself existed, until he'd proven me wrong.

I was pleased to know I was right, after all.

I held out a hand. "Rock me to sleep?"

The door burst open and Toodles streaked through the bedroom. The beast sailed through the air and landed at the foot of the bed. The structure shuddered under the weight of her.

Alaric smirked. "Looks like you have a volunteer."

I gaped at the bed. "Toodles, you take up more than half the bed!"

Alaric patted the beast's head. "Be a good girl and sleep in your own bed."

I shot him a quizzical look. "She has her own bed?"

"She has her own room."

179

And here I thought I couldn't love him any more than I already did.

Toodles slunk from the bedroom, willing but unhappy about the request.

I climbed into bed and patted the empty space next to me. Alaric slid in beside me and I curled against his chest. The longer I stayed, the harder it was to picture myself on the road without him. The harder it also was to keep secrets from him.

"Do you know anything about prophecies?"

He propped himself up on one elbow. "That's a very broad question. A specific prophecy?"

"One about the return of the sun."

"There are prophecies about that? I suppose it doesn't surprise me. There's a prophecy for everything, really, and that one's a pretty big deal." He laughed. "I once had a seer tell me that I was destined to bring about the downfall of my species. How would one vampire manage such an impressive feat when it took ten supervolcanoes to raise us up?"

"What if I told you I'm part of one of those prophecies?"

He laughed again. "To bring back the sun? Is there a flying chariot in your closet that you haven't told me about?"

"I'm supposedly three points of a triangle."

"Not a love triangle, I hope. Those are terrible."

I couldn't resist a smile. "Not a love triangle. A trinity, if you will."

His mouth quirked. "How holy of you."

I lightly punched his bare chest. "I didn't make the prophecy."

His smile faded. "You're serious."

"I am."

"Where did you learn this—the wise woman you met?"

"That part doesn't matter." I was willing to confess my own secret, but I wasn't willing to invoke Olis—not while the House had a major security issue to resolve. Afterward I'd persuade Olis to come clean about his involvement with the Big Apple wizards and let Alaric decide his fate. I felt strongly that the king wouldn't kill Olis. The wizard had done far more good than harm for the crown and Alaric would take that into account.

"And how do you accomplish this great feat?"

I shrugged. "I didn't ask for the details."

"Why not? I'd want to know."

"For starters, I'm not a believer in prophecies. I think they were mostly created to give hope to people who had none."

He stroked my cheek with his thumb. "Is that such a bad thing?"

"No, of course not."

He scrutinized me. "But there's more."

I wasn't sure how to articulate my feelings. "I don't want to be..."

"Important? Special? Face it, Britt. You're important whether you're part of a prophecy or not."

Now it was my turn to laugh. "Important to whom? I was expelled from my coven, then an assassin. After that an indentured servant. I don't know who I am now." My days of freedom were too few and far between to make a determination.

Alaric traced a line from my lips to chin to my collarbone and it took all my strength not to shudder in response. "You're important to me, Britt. Doesn't that mean anything to you?"

I sighed. "Of course it does." More than I cared to

admit. "Would you still feel that way if I told you I've come around to the idea of hope?"

His brow furrowed. "What do you mean?"

"When I went through the tunnels with Olis, I saw the horrible conditions those people are living in, and I realized how much better the world might be with a shining sun." As promised, I didn't name the Hudson settlement, but I wanted to help them all the same.

Alaric offered a sympathetic look. "Life underground isn't an easy one."

"They live there because of vampires," I said. "Their lives aren't easy because of vampires."

"We're not the ones who caused the Great Eruption. We only took advantage of the outcome." He caressed my cheek again. "It will be better when synthetic blood and a vaccine are widely available."

I wasn't convinced. "Great, humans won't be walking juice boxes. What about everybody else? Witches and wizards are basically paid servants to keep plants growing and the earth spinning. They're not free to live their lives as they choose because the earth would die without them. What if they went on strike?"

"What would that do other than show how necessary they are? It wouldn't change the fundamental fact that the only thing that can relieve them of their burden is the sun." He dragged a hand through his hair. "I get it, Britt. I really do. Vampires suck at ruling. Pun intended. If there's a triangle out there that can bring back the sun, I won't stop it."

My mouth dropped open, but no words came out.

Alaric wore a devilish smile. "You look very inviting right now."

"You really wouldn't try to stop the prophecy?"

"I never wanted power; you know that."

"But vampires only thrive because of the Eternal Night. If daylight is restored to the world, life as you know it will cease to exist."

"A natural part of life is change, Britt. That's why it's described as a cycle. Different species are on top of the pyramid at different times in history depending on the circumstances. Even if the sun returns and vampires are sent scurrying back into the shadows, that doesn't mean humans will rise to the top again. It could be their day is done. Maybe this time it will be the wolves that rule the roost."

"Or witches," I murmured.

"I wouldn't mind seeing a witch on top." His smile widened. "Again."

"You're really not upset? You don't think I'm a traitor?"

"It's a prophecy, Britt. There are more of those than I can count. One involves you. One involves me. I don't plan to let them influence my life. If it comes to pass, then I'll deal with the outcome, but I have no intention of borrowing trouble."

I pressed my palms flat against his smooth chest, enjoying the contact. "You really are nothing like your father."

"Please don't make comparisons to my father when we're in bed together."

"Noted."

His hand skimmed my hip. "Now, what were we saying about a witch on top?"

I offered a demure smile. "I'd rather show than tell."

Chapter Thirteen

The House library was located in a former museum
on West Fifty-Third Street. The New York Public
Library building was destroyed by a random fireball
during the Great Eruption. Fortunately, many of the books
survived because they were located offsite and underground.

Liam met us on the sidewalk outside the library. When
he heard about the dragon encounter, he insisted on seeing
me in person—allegedly to check on my well-being, but I
suspected it was more likely to get the gory details.

I was pleased to see George flying above the werewolf's
head. "I wondered where you'd gone."

"You traumatized him with the whole dragon confronta-
tion," Liam said. "He needed comforting."

"I'm so sorry, George." The phoenix came to land on my
shoulder. "He can come in with us, can't he?"

"As long as he doesn't burn any books," Alaric said.

The vampire strode through the entrance and signaled
to the young woman behind the counter. Recognition
flashed in her eyes as her gaze landed on the king.

"Your Majesty, this is quite an honor," she said, lowering her gaze to the floor.

"Are you the librarian?" he asked.

"No, I'm only a clerk. Jane is in her office." She motioned to the right toward the back of the building. "She's in there now if you want to see her."

"Thank you."

"Normally we don't allow pets in the building," the clerk began.

George made a disgruntled noise.

"This is Sir George," Alaric interjected. "He comes with us."

"Of course. Whatever you desire, Your Majesty." The clerk tilted her head slightly, exposing the curve of her neck. "I'm happy to assist you with anything you might need while you're here, Your Majesty. Anything at all."

"That's very kind. We may take you up on that." Alaric continued in the direction the clerk indicated and I followed suit.

"I think she meant more than research," I whispered. "You shouldn't have sounded so eager."

"You sound awfully jealous for someone who isn't staying."

"She isn't marriage potential."

He grunted. "Now you sound like my mother. Please don't."

The librarian looked up from her desk when we entered. Her pen clattered to the floor, and she stumbled to her feet in an effort to curtsy.

"No formalities, please," Alaric said. "We have an urgent research project. Would you be able to assist with that?"

The librarian's eyes sparkled. "Urgent research? Yes, Your Majesty. Of course. It's what I was born to do."

You had to appreciate a woman with a true calling.

"We're looking for information on a god or goddess and an enchanted suit of armor that belonged to their lover," I explained. "We don't know names. The armor is made from Damascus steel."

Jane blinked rapidly. "Damascus steel? Isn't that a myth?"

"Apparently not," the king said.

"The armor was broken into seven pieces," I continued. "We believe monsters were tasked with finding the scattered pieces and there's a guardian looking after the collected pieces." Or was.

Her head bobbed with such force, I worried it might fall off. "That sounds fascinating."

"If you can point us in the direction of the right stacks, we'd like to help," Alaric told her.

"Oh, we don't keep stacks anymore, Your Majesty. The books are stored elsewhere and brought to a private reading room."

He frowned. "No one browses? I thought browsing was a thing that happened in libraries."

"Not for many years, Your Majesty. At least not here." Jane typed on her computer keyboard with enthusiastic strokes. "I'll make a list of starting points for us."

"Any chance I can get a beverage while we're waiting?" Liam asked. "I rushed over here without eating breakfast."

"No food or drinks in the library," Jane said firmly, rising to her feet. "No exceptions."

Alaric offered a charming smile. "I'm sure you can..."

"No exceptions," Jane repeated. She swept past us to the lobby. "This way to the reading room, please."

Liam and I exchanged glances.

"I like her," Alaric said in a quiet voice.

We gathered around a rectangular table in the reading room and awaited the results of Jane's search. Dozens of books were brought into the room by Jane, the clerk, and a third member of staff. The clerk made a point of placing all her deliveries directly in front of Alaric. I watched her with amusement. The king barely looked up from the open book in front of him. Whatever he was reading had fully absorbed his attention.

Jane eventually joined us, flipping through index after index with surprising speed. "I initially trained to be a lawyer," she said by way of explanation.

Hours went by in mutual silence as we scanned the contents of the books. Once in a while someone would read a passage aloud and then we'd collectively determine its irrelevance.

Jane pounded her fist on a page. "I've got something."

Alaric stood behind her to read over her shoulder. "Anat?"

"Mistress of the Gods," Jane said. "She's been compared with Ishtar, Aphrodite, and Athena."

"Why do you think she's the one?" I asked.

"Armor for one thing. She was a warrior goddess, often depicted in a helmet," Jane explained. "She was known as a defender of cities and a dragon slayer."

"Could've used her yesterday," Alaric remarked.

"Anything about a lover?" I asked.

Jane offered a tiny smile. "She's a goddess. The list tends to be long where they're concerned."

"Lucky," Liam muttered under his breath.

"This is promising." Jane scanned the page. "Her consort was a god sometimes linked to the Egyptian god,

Set." Jane frowned. "There aren't any details given here, only references to other texts." She started to rifle through the pile of books. "Here we go. This one isn't in English, but I should be able to translate."

"I know who Set is," Alaric said. "In Egyptian mythology, Osiris was the Egyptian god of the underworld who was murdered by his jealous brother, Set."

"Osiris is also the god of death and resurrection," Jane added as she flicked through the pages. Her forehead creased as she read.

"What is it?" I prompted.

"According to this text, it was actually the reverse. Osiris was jealous of his brother's relationship with Anat, and violently murdered him."

"As opposed to peacefully murdered?" Liam asked.

Jane puckered her lips. "The translation isn't perfect, but I'm doing my best."

I shot a warning glance at Liam. Sometimes the werewolf was more sarcasm than sense.

"This book states that Anat and Set were deeply in love, but Osiris objected to the match. He worried about the state of the world should those two join forces, so he killed and dismembered his brother, scattering the pieces around the world."

Liam shook his head. "Family, am I right?"

Jane continued to translate. "Seven metal pieces that represented the god were forged by the divine craft-smith god, Credne, at the request of Anat."

"Which explains the Damascus steel," I said.

"The goddess then forced Osiris to use his powers to help her create an enchantment that would resurrect her lover," Jane continued.

Liam scratched his head. "Is body armor a first anniversary gift or fifth? I can never remember."

"It isn't a gift for the living," Jane said. "It's a gift for the dead."

"Wow. She spared no expense," Liam said. "I guess she really loved him."

Slowly Jane raised her head to look at the king. "Once together the fragments of armor can be used to restore Set to life. Osiris pretended to do her bidding, but then scattered the pieces so that Anat couldn't find them. The goddess cast an enchantment over creatures to find the seven pieces and return them to her so she could complete the resurrection."

"Where's Set's spirit in the meantime? Some of kind of purgatory?" Liam asked.

"Possibly," Jane said.

I took a moment to digest the information. "Where is Anat now? We've seen plenty of monsters but no goddess."

"Gods and goddesses no longer inhabit this earthly plane," Jane said. "And even if they did, a goddess wouldn't get her own hands dirty. I suspect she ordered these beasts to find the pieces and put them back together on her behalf."

"And I bet the monsters were dormant until after the Great Eruption," I said. "Maybe they were spat out of one of the supervolcanoes and resumed their duties."

"And the final piece was right here in New York. How lucky for us," Liam remarked. "Set's the Humpty Dumpty of the supernatural world."

I ignored him, intent on continuing Jane's logic. "So the monsters survived and are operating on autopilot because that's what they were ordered to do." That explained why the argus had the strange blue eyes yet still had blood. The giant was following Anat's ancient command just like the keelut and the heart-eater.

"Then the fact that it was a Cor-Comedere seeking out the breastplate really wasn't a coincidence," Alaric said. "It's essentially seeking Set's heart."

Liam whistled. "I'm more interested in the size of his codpiece."

"We know who Osiris is," I said. "What's Set a god of?"

"Puppies and rainbows, obviously," Liam chimed in. He fixed Jane with a pleading look. "Please say puppies and rainbows."

Jane hesitated. "Darkness and evil."

Liam barked a laugh. "I'm no scientist but I think we can agree he's already gotten his way."

Alaric gave him a long look. "Ahem."

Liam cringed. "Right. Sorry, Your Majesty."

"There's more you should know," Jane said. "The enchanted armor makes him invincible to earthly weapons."

"So if the god manifests, he'll be unstoppable," Alaric murmured.

I clenched my hands into fists. "Then we have to make sure that doesn't happen. How do we stop it?"

"That's easy. You keep the seven pieces away from each other," Jane advised.

Alaric, Liam, and I exchanged guilty looks.

"And what if that ship has sailed?" I asked.

Her eyes rounded. "All the pieces have been collected?"

"We have them in the compound," Alaric admitted.

Jane winced. "Then I'm afraid the ball has been set in motion. According to the translation, the best way to kill him now is to let him reform."

"The best way?" I queried.

Her gaze drifted up from the book. "The only way."

"Figures," Liam muttered.

I wasn't a fan of the solution. "You just said the armor is impervious to earthly weapons. If we let the god reform, how can we kill him? He'll have godly powers and we'll have..." I surveyed the room for anything close to a godly power.

"Beer?" Liam offered.

I returned my attention to Jane. "Is it because the god becomes flesh and blood that we can kill him?" Blood I could work with.

"Let me see..." She resumed reading.

"Here's my question," Liam interrupted. "The fragments are together now, but nothing's happened. Why not?"

Jane shushed him and continued reading. "Because Anat's minions aren't with them. Once her agents are reunited with the seven pieces, it will trigger the resurrection."

"In other words, the blue-eyed monsters will keep coming until the resurrection has been successful," I said.

Jane lowered her gaze to the book. "I'm afraid so."

I rubbed my temples. "Okay, then how do we beat them to it so we can control the outcome?"

"There's a ritual," Jane said.

Liam rolled his eyes. "Why am I not surprised? There's always a ritual."

"So we perform the ritual and resurrect the god of evil and darkness," I said. "Then what?"

Jane chewed her lip as she read. "Then you can deliver him to an otherworldly realm for judgment. The realm will appear once the spell is complete. There seems to be a time element involved, but it's difficult to understand."

"Which part of the city would be large enough to house

an entire otherworldly dimension that appears out of nowhere?" I asked.

"It's a hidden realm, don't forget," Jane said. "It might not be easy to pinpoint."

"Hidden from us as a parallel universe-type deal or simply hidden from view?" I pressed.

Jane bit her lip, uncertain.

"The tunnels?" Liam offered. "Plenty of room beneath the city."

Possible but unlikely. "Too many people live down there."

"It seems there will be rivers involved, but I don't quite understand." The librarian looked at Alaric. "I'm sorry, Your Majesty. I wish I could do better."

"You've been an amazing help, Jane," he assured her.

My breathing hitched as I thought of the one place in the city that made sense. "Central Park."

"You're telling me we'll need to take the god to the park?" Liam groaned. "Oh, sure. We'll just invite him for a picnic. Easy peasy."

"It's the only place in the city that could produce an otherworldly realm with rivers." I turned to Jane. "Does it say anything about how we entice the god to join us for a leisurely stroll in the park while we plot to destroy him?"

She followed the text with her finger. "There's a spell that sort of freezes the god. Contains him until he can be delivered to the judges." She grimaced. "Sorry, the translation is murky."

"What's the spell?" Alaric asked.

"It doesn't say specifically." She stopped reading and looked up at us. "It's contained in a separate text called the Book of Fire and Light."

"Is that a problem?" I asked.

Her laughter turned into a snort. "There's only one of that particular book in the whole world."

Alaric eyed her. "And let me guess, it isn't here."

"No, Your Majesty." She bowed her head, as though personally responsible for the location of the book. "As far as I know, the book is housed in the Britannia Library."

"In Britannia City?" Alaric asked.

She nodded. "It's been there since before the Great Eruption."

Alaric's face hardened. "That makes things slightly tricky."

"What's the issue?" I asked.

Alaric heaved a sigh. "I'll have to go through Prince Maeron for a request like this."

"Is that bad?" I asked. "Just explain that this affects all of us, including House Lewis."

He drummed his fingers on the table. "You don't know Maeron. He's a wily one. If I request a favor, he'll demand one in return."

"Kind of worth it, don't you think?"

He looked me in the eye. "Depends on the favor."

"The book would be incredibly old," the librarian interrupted. "It wouldn't surprise me to learn that it's too delicate to travel. You wouldn't want the pages to disintegrate en route."

"No, definitely not," I agreed. "What language is it written in? Do we need a translator?"

"Oh, I can do that for you," Jane offered.

"We'll certainly take you up on that." Alaric started to gather the books off the table.

"I beg your pardon, Your Majesty, but what do you think you're doing?"

Alaric gazed at the librarian with an innocent expression. "What do you mean? I'm taking the relevant books to the compound."

She rested a hand on top of the pile. "I'm afraid these can't leave the premises. They're labeled as resource materials, which means they can't be checked out."

Alaric stared at her. "But I'm the king."

"And these books were here before you and they'll be here long after you. My job is to protect them."

His body went rigid with tension, prompting me to intervene. "Jane, I understand your loyalty to the books, I really do, but this is sort of a dire situation. You've been listening, right? You understand what we're up against? If this god of darkness and evil manifests, the only thing left on earth will be books and no one here to read them. What's the point of that?"

"Books without readers?" Her hand flew to press against her chest and I thought she might need someone to fetch her smelling salts.

"I know. A terrible fate," Alaric said.

Jane quickly pulled herself together. "I'll make an allowance for the king, but I need you to make a list of the books you're removing."

"We will. Thank you, Jane," Alaric said.

She fished through her pockets and produced square scraps of paper and a pencil the size of my thumb. "Write down the title and number for each book you take."

"No problem." I took the pencil and paper and started logging the information.

We had to get that book from House Lewis. If Anat's plan was successful, the god of darkness would be revived and destroy the world.

No pressure.

Chapter Fourteen

"You're staying for the call, aren't you?" Alaric asked. The two of us had disappeared into his office at the compound following our library visit.

"The call with House Lewis?"

He nodded. "I could use the moral support."

I smiled. "What's the problem with this guy?"

"He's sketchy," Alaric said.

I climbed onto his lap. "Sketchier than you? I find that hard to believe."

"You trust me, though. You wouldn't trust him."

I gazed into his eyes. "You seem to have forgotten our prior history."

He brushed his lips against mine. "I'm happy to apologize again if you've forgotten how sorry I am."

I angled my head to give him access to my neck. "I do like your apologies. They're very sexy."

"I don't think apologies are supposed to be sexy," he murmured as his lips blazed a trail down the curve of my neck.

I didn't acknowledge the sound of a clearing throat until the third time. I knew it was Olis the first two times and I thought it would be fun to see the lengths he'd go to in order to get our attention. Apparently, he was content with various degrees of throat clearing.

"Olis, come in." Alaric waved the wizard forward.

"House Lewis is ready on their end. If you need to postpone, Your Majesty, I can come back."

I slid off the king's lap. "We're ready."

Olis faced the empty space across from the king's desk and moved his left hand in a circular motion. Golden light sparked from his fingertips and the air grew thick with static. Finally, the image of a vampire became clear. I wasn't sure why, but I expected Maeron to look more like a troll than a dark-haired, handsome prince with olive skin and inviting pink lips. His eyes were his most interesting feature. They were like two dark pools that enticed you while they also threatened to drown you.

"King Alaric." He spoke with an accent, which shouldn't have surprised me, yet it did.

Alaric offered a royal nod. "Prince Maeron."

"We were dreadfully sorry to hear about your father's passing."

"Thank you. It was painfully unexpected."

"How can House Lewis be of service to you?"

"We're in need of a book that we understand is located in your library."

The prince smiled, and I caught a glimpse of a gemstone that adorned one of his fangs. "We have many libraries here, Your Majesty. You'll have to be more specific."

"Britannia Library. The tome is called the Book of Fire and Light."

The prince spoke to someone out of view. A moment later he returned his attention to Alaric. "It seems that particular tome is housed in our rare books section. I'll have one of the witches on staff manifest a replica of the book so you can read it, but I'm afraid I can't allow you to have the physical copy. Our Head Librarians would go ballistic if it left the building."

"I understand," Alaric said. "As long as we can read it, I think that's the crucial part."

"Very well then. I'll make the arrangements."

"Thank you."

"An interesting book. May I ask why you're in need of it?"

I knew we were unlikely to get off the hook that easily.

Alaric slotted his fingers together in a calm gesture. "I'm afraid it's a matter of House security."

"A threat to your House or a threat to all Houses?" Maeron asked. I had to give him credit, the prince was as sharp as his fangs.

"That remains to be seen," Alaric replied. "For the time being, it only concerns House August. Should the threat prove greater, you'll be the first to know."

"I'd expect nothing less. You need the replica urgently then?"

"We do."

"Then you shall have it immediately."

"Thank you, Your Highness. House August offers its gratitude." Alaric nodded to Olis, and the wizard broke the connection.

"He'll want more than gratitude," Olis remarked.

Alaric shrugged. "It could've been worse."

"We'll have a copy of the book," Olis said. "That's the important thing, Your Majesty."

"It is."

I smiled at Alaric. "You sounded slightly more regal when you spoke to him. Was that deliberate?"

Alaric's brow wrinkled. "Regal? I'm the king. Don't I always sound regal?"

"Not like that. Any further conversation and you'd have busted out a 'shall' and 'henceforth.'"

Alaric narrowed his eyes. "You know how I adore it when you mock me, especially in front of staff."

"Olis doesn't mind, do you?" I turned my smile to the wizard.

"I rather enjoy it," Olis said.

Alaric made a noise of disgust. "You're going to persuade the entire region to disrespect me."

I pressed my finger against the tip of his nose. "Never, Your Majesty."

Laughter escaped Olis and he quickly covered it with a cough. "If you're no longer in need of me, Your Majesty, I'll help prepare the room for the librarian. I'd like to see that she has everything she needs to perform any necessary translations."

"Thank you, Olis. That would be helpful."

"It's nice to see Houses cooperating," I said, once the wizard vacated the room.

"What do you mean? You saw us cooperate with House Nilsson not so long ago."

"That's true. I hope it's a new trend."

He frowned. "Why does it matter? I would think you'd prefer us to tear each other to pieces."

I cupped his cheeks in my hands. "Not you, Your Majesty. I never want anything bad to happen to you even if that means all the royal vampires in the world join forces."

"That's very sweet. And very uncharacteristic."

I planted a firm kiss on his lips. "I want to know you're safe, Alaric. That's why I'm here."

"And here I thought you stayed to protect the city."

I pressed my forehead against his. "Haven't you figured it out yet? The city is you, Your Majesty. I'm here for you."

"Still have that suitcase packed?" Alaric asked.

"I haven't exactly had time to unpack it now, have I?"

His eyes blazed with hope. "Does that mean you're reconsidering?"

"I don't think it's wise to make important decisions when under life-or-death stress."

"Fair enough." Alaric's lips met mine. They seemed softer somehow, as though time and circumstance had weathered them. "Good luck with the ritual. Come back to me in one piece."

Always, I thought but couldn't bring myself to say it out loud. I wasn't in the habit of making promises I couldn't keep.

Olis wisely arranged for the ritual to take place in the keep. With no windows, massive stone walls, and restricted access, the octagonal keep was the most secure room in the compound. The wizard also wisely arranged to be outside the keep with a group of guards while Liam, Jane, and I handled the ritual inside.

"Let's go through this one more time," Liam said, once he'd placed the seven fragments of armor on the floor inside the summoning circle.

"Lots of 'R's. Ritual. Resurrect. Repatriate," I said.

Liam's brow wrinkled. "Repatriate?"

I shrugged. "Banishment, but I wanted another 'R' word."

He rubbed the back of his neck. "Are you sure we don't need dynamite? It isn't too late, you know."

I patted his cheek. "No earthly weapons include dynamite."

He tilted his head from one side to the other, stretching his neck muscles as though preparing to run a race. "I'd feel better with a small bag of explosives. They're like my security blanket."

"Relax. It's just a ritual."

"No, it's a potential apocalypse that will make the Great Eruption look like an opening act."

Right.

I turned to face the altar where the Book of Fire and Light replica now shimmered. "How's it going, Jane?"

The librarian gazed at the book's image in reverence. "Gorgeous, isn't it? A shame I can't hold the real thing. I'd love to visit the Britannia Library one day, although I doubt I'll get the chance."

"The king will owe you after this. Maybe he can arrange it."

Jane broke into a nervous smile. "This is the most exciting project I've ever undertaken."

"I'm glad one of us is excited." On the scale of excitement to dread, I was somewhere around nauseated. If we couldn't decode the spell or we made a mistake, we risked plummeting the world into chaos and destruction. If we didn't beat the arrival of Anat's minions, we also lose. The responsibility weighed heavily on me.

Liam clapped his hands once. "It's now or never. Are we ready?"

Nodding, Jane began to read aloud from the book. I didn't understand a word of it, not that it mattered. The important part was the metal monster of evil we were summoning.

Inside the chalk circle, the pieces of armor vibrated. One by one they drifted into the air as though controlled by an unseen hand. Brilliant light emanated from them.

The walls shook, knocking debris to the floor. Liam and I exchanged alarmed glances. The monsters had found us.

Jane paused to observe the mess.

"Keep going," I urged.

She picked up where she left off. The seven fragments shifted to position themselves in the right order. A shadow rose from the floor like a cloud of ash. The walls shook again.

Jane's face drained of color. "Great gods above."

I spun toward her. "What's wrong?"

"The book. I need the book!"

I gestured to the shimmering item on the altar. "You have the book."

"No, I mean the actual book. I misinterpreted one of the phrases, which is very easy to do, by the way. No one speaks this language anymore and they haven't for thousands of years."

"Okay, no need to get snippy. Why do you need the physical book?"

The words tumbled from her lips at a rapid pace. "The first spell resurrects him. The second spell banishes him into the book itself to allow you to transport him to the other realm for judgment. That's how you're able to deliver him."

My heart stuttered. "No book. No banishment."

Her eyes radiated fear. "Exactly."

Without a physical copy, the invincible god would stay right here on earth and destroy us all. "We need to tell the king."

Her fingers trembled as she turned the page. "There isn't time. Even if he can get in touch with House Lewis right away, he won't be able to get his hands on the book as quickly as we need it."

Liam gaped at the rising shadow. "Whatever you need to do, do it fast."

"Stay here!" I yanked open the door and ran from the keep to find Alaric.

Olis emerged from behind a row of guards that blocked my path. "What are you doing up here?" he demanded.

"I need Alaric...the king," I said, quickly correcting myself in front of so many of his vampire guards.

"We discussed this," Olis began. "His Majesty is to remain protected during the ritual in case something goes awry."

"Something *has* gone awry. Tell him we need the physical book. He needs to contact House Lewis *right now* and find a way to get it to us before we all die."

I spun on my heel and ran back to the keep. If the god snapped on those pieces of armor before the book arrived... It didn't bear thinking about.

I slammed the door behind me upon reentering the keep. Liam pointed to the far wall with the tip of his broadsword. "Something's digging over there."

I followed his gaze to where dirt and rocks sprayed in all directions. A keelut.

"You're up, Liam." I had to stay focused on the developing god.

"This one's a beheading, right?" he asked.

I nodded as a keelut emerged from the floor in all its hairless dog-spirit glory.

The werewolf raised his sword. "It's a dog-eat-dog world we live in."

The wall to my right burst open and a Cor-Comedere tore through the gaping hole. I kicked a crossbow from the floor into my awaiting hands and took a shot. The bolt buried itself in the supernatural monster's eye. I reloaded and shot again. The heart-eater dissipated in a blaze of blue light.

"How are they getting in?" Liam asked as he dispatched the keelut.

"The same way they did last time. They're supernatural with the power of an ancient goddess."

Liam gestured to the side of the room where golden light sparked. "Uh, what's happening over there?"

Golden light didn't herald one of Anat's monsters. This was something else. The light glowed brighter as it formed a circle.

Terrific, the god decided to bring a friend.

Sweat streaked Liam's face as he glanced from the emerging god to the growing portal. "What do we do?"

I pivoted to face the portal. "I'll grab hold of whatever this is before it can do any damage." Only Set would be wearing enchanted armor. All bets were off for the companion.

Another Cor-Comedere broke through the wall and went straight for Liam. Stones scattered to the floor and joined the rest of the rubble.

An amorphous body began to fill the armor. Set was almost here.

A short silhouette appeared in the golden portal like a black hole on the face of the sun.

"Special delivery," a voice chirped. A petite blonde emerged from the portal brandishing a book.

The Book.

Her gaze darted around the keep and she seemed to

realize she'd arrived during a crucial moment. Her eyes shone with anticipation.

"Davina, move faster!" another voice shouted. "You're blocking the way."

Davina? I took in the young vampire's pale pink magical armor and matching pink boots. Chimera on a cracker. Princess Davina of House Lewis was delivering the book by hand.

Davina spared a glance over her shoulder. "They're already slaying monsters, London. Hurry!" She sounded far too enthusiastic.

A second woman emerged from the portal. Her jet-black hair was secured in a long braid, and she was dressed in a dark blue outfit paired with boots. "Monsters? Perfect timing."

Davina searched the room. "Which one of you is the librarian?"

Jane popped up from behind the altar and raised her hand. The vampire princess tossed the book to Jane, who caught it and immediately ducked behind the altar again.

London released a shrill whistle and more women poured out of the portal. Each one wore the same dark blue liquid armor. The suits reminded me of what Genevieve and Michael wore in our battle against the Pey.

"That portal is like a clown car for hot witches," Liam observed. "Any hot wizards in there?"

"We're knights," London shot back.

"I'm not," Davina said. She raised her sword. "But I fight like one."

There were six arrivals in total.

"Wow. Is that Damascus steel?" a red-haired knight asked as she observed the summoning circle.

My head swiveled toward her. "You know about Damascus steel?"

"An ancient metal. Very powerful," the redhead said. "Impervious to fire. Malleable."

"And enchanted," I breathed. Even with the extra help, this fight wasn't going to be easy. I hoped the spell worked or everybody in this room was doomed. Hell, everybody in this world was doomed.

Davina cut a glance at the shadow and armor. "This is the god?"

"Almost," I told her.

"Why not kill him now before he reforms?" a stocky blonde asked.

"We need to resurrect him. It's the only way to send him packing for good," I explained.

The keep seemed to tilt on its axis as monsters flooded the room. So much for Olis and his wards. I felt overwhelmed by the sheer number of them in the enclosed space. Even if we stopped the god, we might succumb to his protectors.

"Kami, behind you!" London yelled.

A keelut attacked the stocky blonde. "Kill that one with magic or behead it!" I called. "Those are the options."

The knights fought like a trained unit, and I felt a momentary pang of envy. I'd mainly fought alone or as an outcast. Even as part of the security team, the majority of my assignments had been solitary. These witches clearly had fought alongside each other for long enough to anticipate each other's moves. What a luxury.

I shook off my moment of self-pity and let them work defense while I ran behind the table to check on Jane's progress.

The librarian was tracing a sentence with her fingers and mouthing each word.

"Rehearsal time is over, Jane," I told her. "In case you haven't noticed, the show's already started."

Jane turned to me with tears in her eyes. "I can't do it, Britt. What if I make another mistake? The fate of the world rests on how well I perform this spell."

"And if you don't perform, we know what that fate will be."

Jane seemed to fold in on herself. Good grief. Now wasn't the time to fall apart.

I peered around the table to see another knight dispatch two monsters at once. Impressive.

I joined Jane on the floor. "Tell me what to do and I'll do it."

Jane seemed to regain her composure. "No, I'm fine now. I can do it. I'm so sorry. I won't let you down."

A heart-eater lunged at me from the side. I punched its snout and tried to block its path to Jane and the book. I didn't have to kill it. I only needed to buy the librarian time.

The air swirled in the room. I held up my arms to block a flying sword from hitting me in the face. The hilt smashed into my wrist and fell to the floor.

"I have been reborn!" a voice boomed.

The moment of truth had arrived.

"All that translating and he speaks English?" Jane complained. She held open the book and began the incantation.

Set rose to his full height, taller and broader than a mighty oak. His head skimmed the ceiling of the keep. I tried to form a connection with his blood, but I couldn't seem to penetrate the enchanted armor to reach it.

"He looks strong," Liam observed.

"You thought he'd be a little lamb?" Kami shot back.

"Lamb? Great, now I'm hungry," Liam grumbled.

Kami grinned as she pulled her blade from the belly of a heart-eater. "I like you already."

The keep filled with blue light as the remaining monsters dissipated. With the creatures gone, the knights surrounded the god. They might not be able to kill him, but they could keep him occupied while Jane finished the spell.

The god seemed to sense Jane was the one to eliminate. His tree-limb of an arm swept three of the knights aside as he attempted to leave the circle.

I threw myself between the god and the altar. Set's eyes met mine and a horrible sensation overtook me. Darkness and evil were no exaggeration. I felt like I was falling backward into a pit of despair.

Jane screamed a word I didn't understand.

As the god raised his arm to knock me aside, his body took on the appearance of impressionist artwork. Blurred and broken colors filled the spaces between the metal fragments. The god broke into a cloud of colorful dust. I ducked as the cloud traveled over my head to the book. The moment the last molecule entered the book, Jane slammed it closed and leaned on top of it.

"Got him," she said, panting.

Liam ran to the chalk circle and collected the pieces of metal scattered across the floor. "We sent the god of darkness to be judged but got to keep his invincible armor? Score!"

"I'll have Alaric keep it somewhere safe and secret," I said. "I wouldn't want word to get out there's an invincible suit of armor up for grabs."

Liam clutched the breastplate to his chest. "Invisible would be better."

I cut him a quizzical look. "You think invisible would be better than invincible?"

"If they can't see me, they probably won't be able to kill me either, so it ends up being both."

I shook my head. "Your logic is truly astounding sometimes."

London appeared beside me. "I take it he doesn't stay in the book. What's the next step?"

"We need to deliver the book to an otherworldly realm for judgment," I said.

"Sounds fun," a slender witch with pink tipped-dark hair said. "Count me in."

"Please say the monsters are done," the redhead said. "I don't care if the keeluts are hairless. I think I'm allergic." She sneezed.

"Don't worry," I told them. "The next part will be a walk in the park."

Chapter Fifteen

W e stood on the sidewalk and contemplated the murky expanse. Between the keep and Central Park, I managed to learn the names of our rescue squad. Davina aside, they were collectively known as the Knights of Boudica. London, Kami, Ione, Briar, and Stevie were in attendance and each one possessed a different set of magical skills. According to Kami, they'd left two knights behind at their headquarters in Britannia City.

"Why is this called a park?" Kami asked as we ventured forward with flashlights blazing. "It's nothing but a giant swamp."

"Like the parks in Britannia City are better?" Ione asked.

We passed a large statue covered in green slime. I was surprised to find it still in one piece. The air reeked of moisture and decay.

Liam craned his neck. "Who's got the book?"

"Still me," I said, reaching over my shoulder to pat the backpack.

"Okay, just checking again. Don't want to wade into the swamp unnecessarily."

"What did you say you fought in here before?" London asked me.

"Two-headed serpent. About yay big." I raised a hand high above my head. "Called a bitie."

"Even if we don't see serpents, I bet there are plenty of other monsters crawling around in here," Davina said.

The redhead named Briar looked at her. "You sound a little too hopeful."

"I knew I should've brought my explosives," Liam complained. "We could've cleared a path straight to the hidden realm."

"You can't clear a path to a hidden realm if you don't know where it is," I pointed out. I hacked at the dark vines along the way and steered clear of the mud. It wasn't easy.

Liam sniffed the air. "I smell water."

Kami snorted. "Look around. There's water all around us." She lifted a boot to show the mud caked to the bottom.

"No, this is different. It's not stagnant," Liam explained.

"He's right," Stevie said. "I should know. I'm a water witch."

Jane said there'd be rivers. "Take us to it," I ordered.

I fell back and let Stevie take the lead. She trudged forward with an air of authority. The rest of us fanned out behind her.

I had no sense of how far we'd traveled into the park when we reached the bank of a fast-moving body of water.

"It's a river," Liam said.

"And the award for Most Obvious Statement goes too..." Kami swept an arm in the werewolf's direction.

He grinned at her. "I think we might be soulmates—in the platonic sense."

Kami scrunched her nose. "Is there a platonic version?"

"Sure there is," Liam said. "Don't you know any ancient Greek?"

Briar's hands moved to her hips as she contemplated the flowing water. "Okay, we found a river. Do we set sail or cross it or what?"

I observed the current. "We take it." I wasn't sure how I knew, but I did.

"If it's anything like the river Styx, we need a boat," London said.

Kami scanned the area. "Anybody see a boat?"

"The only thing I see is increased exposure to disease," Liam replied. He smacked his arm. "Liam: twelve. Mosquitoes: five."

"They must like you," I told him. "I haven't been bitten at all."

He scratched his arm. "That's because I'm taking all the hits for you.

"Give me one second to sort this out." Stevie concentrated on the water.

I watched as the current slowed.

"What's your plan?" Liam asked. "Drain it so we can walk?"

"He's right. We still need a ride," Kami said.

Briar waded into the water. "I can help with that." She closed her eyes and focused.

Liam leaned over to Kami and whispered, "She's going to build a boat with her mind?"

"Just wait," Kami replied.

The witch's body stretched, widened, and hardened into a rowboat large enough to accommodate our party.

Liam and I wore matching gobsmacked expressions.

"Turns out our shapeshifter witch can replicate more than animals," Kami said. "All aboard Briar."

"I've never heard of a shapeshifter witch," I said as I climbed into the boat.

"She uses chaos magic," London explained. "It's pretty wild. You should've seen her practice sessions."

Liam lifted up a foot and stared at the bottom of the boat. "I hope I'm not stepping on any sensitive parts."

Kami pushed him to a seated position. "Stop fretting and sit."

I joined Liam on the bench as the boat surged ahead. For a brief moment, I forgot all about the monumental task at hand and simply enjoyed the wind on my face.

All at once the flashlights dimmed.

Liam's voice cut through the stunned silence. "Um, anybody else get the distinct sense of foreboding?"

He wasn't wrong. My skin pricked with anticipation. After a moment, my eyes adjusted to the lack of light and a familiar face glowed in the darkness across from me. Her name blazed in my mind like someone had branded it there.

Jocelyn Thomas.

She was my first official hit. According to the client, Jocelyn had a nasty habit of stealing human babies from birthing centers and feeding on them. She left a trail of tiny corpses from Philadelphia to Charlottesville. I found her outside a birthing center in a small town northeast of Charlottesville. She didn't manage to get inside. I was sloppy and inexperienced then. I thought I had to make a statement, so I drained her blood and left her husk of a body exactly where I found it. I might as well have mounted her head on a spike and posted it as a warning to other vampires. The move had been dramatic and unnecessary and made me look like a psychopath who enjoyed killing as much as Jocelyn—which couldn't have been further from the truth.

"What do you see?" Liam whispered.

"Nothing," I said, a little too quickly. "Why? What do you see?"

"An ex-boyfriend."

"Matt?"

He looked at me with a soulful expression. "You remember?"

"How could I forget?" Liam was in dire straits the day I moved into the apartment building and Matt had been a major reason for it. I basically talked the werewolf out of killing himself.

Liam exhaled softly. "You are so much kinder than you realize."

"I see an outfit I adored when I was young and stupid," Kami shared.

Liam craned his neck to look at her. "An outfit? There's a floating pile of clothes out there in the shadows?"

"Oh, I'm wearing the outfit," Kami admitted. She stared at an image only she could see. "I don't know how I ever thought that was flattering on me."

"I know where we are," London said. "It's Cocytus, the river of lamentation."

"Is that important?" Liam asked.

"It suggests we're on the right path," London replied.

"I can still see images when I close my eyes," Ione complained. "There's no escaping them."

"The river is forcing us to confront our regrets," London told us. "It's a test."

Liam pivoted toward Kami. "If yours is only poor fashion choices, you're doing well."

Kami's tense expression suggested otherwise.

"Why do you know so much about this?" I asked London.

"My mother taught history and she made it a priority to pass as much of her knowledge on to me as she possibly could."

"Be sure to tell her thanks when you get back. It might just save our lives."

London's expression softened. "If I'm able to tell her thanks in person, it means we failed."

"I'm sorry," I said.

"It could be worse," Stevie piped up. "We could be on Acheron."

"What's Acheron?" Liam asked.

London's expression turned somber. "The river of pain."

The sound of rushing water drew my attention ahead. "Don't speak so soon. The river's about to divide."

Davina grabbed the edge of the boat. "And it's picking up speed."

Stevie patted the side of the boat. "Be careful, Briar."

The boat shot toward the center of the divide, seemingly unable to control the direction. As we reached the split, the boat tipped to the right and I gripped the seat to keep myself from falling overboard. Water splashed us as the boat returned to a normal position and jerked to the left. The current swept us forward at a rapid rate.

"Oh, no." London wiped the damp from her eyes. "We're missing a few."

Ione, Davina, and Stevie had been dumped from the boat.

Kami looked behind us. "They seem to have been taken in another direction."

"Taken?" I echoed.

"The river decided," London said. "We continue this way and they go..." She motioned to the opposite direction. "That way."

"Why?" I asked.

"I'm not sure, but I assume it will become clear eventually," London said.

"As long as we're going to the good place and not the river of pain," Liam remarked. He looked at the remaining occupants of the boat. "Okay, I'm going to have to revise that theory."

"What about the others?" I asked. "We've got the boat."

"Ione's an earth witch and Stevie's a water witch," Kami said. "They'll be fine."

But would we?

We sat in contemplative silence, no doubt trying to figure out to which river we'd been subjected.

Liam finally broke the silence. "Nothing's happening. That's good, right?"

London scanned the water below. "I don't know about good, but it means we're probably not on Acheron."

"I hope the others aren't either," Kami said.

"What are the other options?" I asked.

London gazed at the black water. "I think this is Lethe, the river of oblivion. If you drink from these waters, you'll forget."

"Forget what?" Liam asked. "If it's my most embarrassing moments, I'll need an extra-large cup."

"You forget the suffering you endured while you lived, but you also forget all you've done." London looked at me. "Tempting, isn't it?"

I considered the rippling water, remembering all the tablet in the Archive Room had shown me. "Yes and no." I'd endured terrible things and done worse. To forget them would be a blessing and yet...

"I don't want to forget any of it," I announced. Without the expulsion from the coven and my parents' rejection, I wouldn't have become an assassin. But I also wouldn't have met George. And I wouldn't have become an indentured servant to House August. I wouldn't have met Alaric or Liam. Each negative experience had a positive one attached to it. Even the most painful moments had meaning. They'd shaped me into the witch I was today.

Liam leaned over the side of the boat. "Can we target a specific memory if we only take a sip?"

"I was wondering the same," Kami said.

"You'd better decide quickly," I said, pointing.

Liam turned to look. "There's another fork? Is it a fork if it's not a road?"

There was no time to answer. Once again, the boat tipped right and jerked left. I cleared the water from my eyes to see only London left in the boat with me.

"Do you think they're okay?" I asked.

"I hope so. It was my idea to come to New York. It'll be my fault if anything happens to them."

"Look on the bright side. If we die now, nobody can yell at you later."

London smiled. "I appreciate your sunny optimism."

The water began to burn with white-hot flames. "That can't be good."

London studied the river. "If this is anything like the Phlegethon, I think it might be our last water ride."

"Thank the gods. What's the Phlegm-a-thon?"

"A river of fire usually associated with the Greek underworld, but it's not like we need a Greek passport to enter. At the end of this, we should arrive at some sort of gate where we can deposit our friend in the book."

"Why these rivers when Set isn't Greek?"

"Set isn't Set either."

True. The god had many names and many stories attached to him. The truth was beyond our ken.

"Is Briar okay riding a river of fire? I don't know about you, but my backside is flammable and I'm sure she's not in the mood to become a rump roast."

London peered over the side to examine the boat. "No sign of burnt boat."

"I can't imagine the good souls would be excited about their afterlife at this point." I waved a hand at the fiery water. "They probably wish they'd chosen oblivion."

Flames traveled up the side of the boat and threatened to engulf us. The boat started to constrict, and I realized Briar was about to return to her normal shape. The fire must've been too hot for her.

London and I locked eyes. "What now?" I asked.

"How fast can you swim?"

I twisted to look at the route ahead. "I see land."

London rubbed the side of the boat. "Do what you have to do, Briar. We'll see you on the other side."

The other side of what?

I unhooked the backpack. "I can't let the book get wet."

"What's your plan?"

I judged the distance to shore. "I have a good arm. I can make it."

"I hope you're right or this whole journey was for nothing."

The boat shrank again and tilted to the right. I bolted to my feet and threw the backpack with as much force as I could muster. It sailed through the air and landed on the riverbank with a heavy thud.

Then I jumped.

My skin felt like it was going to melt straight off the bones. Still, I swam. I had to get to the book.

I reached shore and clawed my way up the bank. I was relieved to see London beside me. I struggled to my feet and tried to ignore the shooting pain in my back as I looped on the straps of the backpack.

"There's the gate," London said.

In the distance glowed a large set of golden gates. Almost there.

A bulky silhouette appeared in front of the gates, blotting out a section of the soothing golden glow.

"Please tell me that's a judge coming for the book."

"Sorry. It's a crossroads demon," London said.

My shoulders sagged. "Seriously? We just went through all that and now we have to fight a demon?"

"I think it's the final step before we reach the gate."

The demon lumbered toward us. His three eyes glowed red and he sported spikes along his back and arms. I had no doubt each spike was tipped with poison because why not?

"Why is there only one demon? Seems like they need Olis down here to beef up security."

"You're insulting my skills already?" the demonic porcupine lamented. "At least fight me first."

"You speak English?" I asked.

"I speak every language. It's no fun taunting someone in Russian if they don't speak the language." He cracked his neck. "I miss some of the ancient tongues, though. They had some incredible insults."

"As much as I appreciate a good insult, we're not here to fight," I said.

"Everybody's here to fight. That's the only way you get in."

"We're not staying. We have a delivery." I turned to show him the backpack.

The demon cast a speculative glance at us. "What kind of delivery?"

"A god of darkness desperately in need of judgment," I said. "I think your people have been waiting to sentence him for quite a long time."

The demon appeared intrigued. "I still have to fight you, though. Rules are rules."

I sighed. "This is literally a kill the messenger situation."

"How about this?" the demon proposed. "I'll go easy on you. Take a few swings. Let me hit you and maybe take out a small chunk of flesh." He held his index finger and thumb an inch apart.

"No flesh," I said firmly. "The poison on those spikes will kill us."

The demon rolled his red eyes. "Fine. Be that way."

"We traveled down raging rivers and faced inner demons," I said. "I think it's a bit unfair to expect us to kill an outer one now."

"Kill?" He laughed like it was the funniest joke he'd ever heard. "Nobody kills me."

"We can take you," I said.

London folded her arms and bumped out a hip. "Definitely."

"What makes you so sure?" the demon asked. He sounded more curious than outraged.

"I can control your body."

"And I can control your mind," London added. "Well, technically Kami does mind control. My magic works a

219

little differently." She turned to me. "I can win over animals, which includes most monsters."

I gestured to the demon. "Then you can control this lug, right? He must fall under the monster umbrella."

"Hey," the demon objected. "Who are you calling a lug?"

"I can try."

"On the count of three," I said. "One, two…"

"Three," we said in unison.

My magic penetrated the demon's body.

"Hey, that tickles," he objected, lowering his spiked arms.

A thought nagged at me. "Once we deliver the package, how do we get back?" I asked London. Briar was gone now and our means of transport with her.

"I can create portals. That's how we got to you with the book."

"If you can portal us back, why didn't you portal us to the gates?"

The demon laughed. "Do you really think the judges would let anybody portal directly here? You would've ended up in a desert realm without a drop of water."

London nodded. "What he said."

The demon used a spiky arm to scratch his stomach. "Portal or not, nobody gets back just like nobody kills me. Those gates are a one-way ticket."

Tendrils of my magic sliced through the demon's blood. Although the blood was thicker and required more effort than the usual kind, I managed to slow the flow faster than I expected.

The demon's three eyelids fluttered closed and his body sank to the ground.

"You're welcome," London said.

"What do you mean? I did that."

"Oh, I didn't realize you were doing anything."

I gawked at her. "You said you could win him over. How is that putting him to sleep?"

"I persuaded him to take a nap."

"And I slowed his blood until he passed out." And now I felt ready to pass out.

"I guess he was right about nobody killing him," London said. She sauntered toward the gates.

I hurried to catch up. "Didn't that wear you out?"

"No, I find the use of magic invigorating."

"Lucky you. I'd like a nap." No rest for the wicked, though. Not until the deed was done. We stopped in front of the massive gates. "How do you think it works? We open the book at the gate and let him loose?"

"Not sure yet. In the Greek version, the gates are guarded by Cerberus. You make it past the guardian and then the fate of your soul is determined by three judges. Rhadamanthus, Minos, and Aeacus assess the deeds of your life and pass judgment accordingly."

I grunted. "Gee, I just love the concept of being judged by three dudes, don't you?"

"The Egyptians have forty-two judges."

"That seems like too many chefs in the kitchen."

London laughed. "Is there a magic number you'd be happy with, Goldilocks?"

"Not really. I'm a little squeamish about the whole judgment part in general. I guess it doesn't matter how many there are."

She gave me a long look. "You and me both."

The golden gates parted to admit us. "Do you think the demon was right about this being a one-way ticket?"

London shrugged. "He was right about nobody killing him."

"That was our choice, though." I inclined my head toward the gates. "This is different."

We stared at each other for a long moment.

"I'll go. You stay here," London said. "Give me the book." She held out her hand.

"No, I'll take it," I insisted. "You have the knights. Reasons to live."

"As do you," London replied.

"Alaric's the king. He'll be fine without me."

She smiled. "Perhaps, but he'd be far better with you by his side. Trust me, I know."

I ran through the options in my head. Only one made sense. "You've got the portal magic. The only shot I have at survival is if you hold the portal open for me, but I can't do the same for you. If I'm not back in a reasonable time, then go without me."

London seemed to take the suggestion under advisement. Finally, she nodded. "I'll keep it open for you."

I knew she was only saying that to be kind. It was hard to acknowledge the truth of the matter—that I wouldn't make it back. The Archive Room had shown me a version of myself that I found hard to stomach and I had no doubt the judgment against me would be severe. There was likely no way to deliver Set for judgment without being held accountable for my own transgressions. We'd have to be a package deal. It was a lucky day for the assessors.

I pushed down a wave of nausea. "Tell Alaric...Tell His Majesty that I..." For the first time words failed me.

London seemed to sense my internal struggle. "I will."

I said a silent prayer to the gods and stepped through

the open gates. They slammed closed behind me and I heard the sound of a lock snapping. Nice touch.

The landscape on this side of the gates was completely different from the riverside. A meadow on the horizon shimmered in pastel light.

A statuesque woman came into view. Her brown hair was twisted in a chignon, and she wore floor-length white robes with gold accents. I had no doubt she was a goddess, although I had no idea which one.

"Welcome, Britt Miller."

"Just Britt." I'd left the name Miller behind as a child and never looked back. "I come bearing gifts," I said, and thrust the book toward her.

Her gaze lowered to the offering. "Thank you." The goddess removed the book from my grasp. "Follow me."

I swallowed hard. "Do I have to? My friend is waiting for me outside the gates. She's my ride home."

The goddess said nothing, leaving me no choice but to follow.

We turned left and arrived at an amphitheater built into the ground out of stone and wood and other natural elements. The seats were already filled, no doubt with judges.

The goddess carried the book to the bottom of the amphitheater where the stage was located. She indicated for me to stop at the base and continued onstage. She placed the book on an altar and opened it.

"I summon thee, god of darkness and evil. Appear before us and face your final judgment."

The book glowed with a golden hue and the same hulking figure emerged that I'd glimpsed in the keep.

"Here you will answer for your sins," she said.

"I answer to no one," he bellowed. "I am..." His lips were sewn shut by an unseen hand.

The goddess turned to address a judge in the front row. "Thank you." She continued to read a long list of grievances that seemed to stretch into the next century, but I suspected time worked differently here.

And I thought I was bad. I didn't hold a candle to this god's evildoings. It was a good thing we captured him or the world would've been in peril. Although I knew a certain segment of the population might disagree, Set would've been a far worse option than vampires and this assessment proved it.

The god was sentenced to eternal torment and his body set ablaze. His screams would stay with me for the rest of my mortal life, all two minutes of it, probably. I watched as his form disintegrated amidst a bright blue light. When the fire died, only a small pile of ash remained. A gnome hurried to the stage and swept the debris into a dustpan with a brush. The stage was now ready for its next guest, presumably me.

A lump formed in my throat as I started toward the goddess.

She held up a hand. "Not so quickly, Britt Miller."

"Please don't call me that."

"I am impressed by your sacrifice," the goddess said.

"Oh, are we doing positive impact statements first?" I must've missed the positive remarks about Set.

The goddess regarded me with a vague smile. "You cannot stay here, witch."

"Well, I can't go back according to the rules. Where does that leave me?" I pictured myself like Sisyphus, doomed to be tormented for eternity. What would be my version of pushing a boulder up a hill? I imagined Alaric on an island within view and me, in a boat without oars. I'd try desperately to reach him only to be repeatedly blown off course.

"You have a vivid imagination," the goddess said.

I balked. "You can read my thoughts?"

"Only in here. Once you've left this realm, I no longer have the ability."

"That's good because I..." It took a few seconds for her words to sink in. "Wait. Once I leave this realm?"

"As a reward for your sacrifice, we've decided to allow you to return home," she said. "You're needed far more there than you are here."

My mouth dropped open. "You don't want to send me to the pit of despair or whatever hell you've crafted for the baddies?"

Her smile made me feel like a basket of kittens had been deposited on my doorstep. "The world isn't finished with you yet, Britt the Blood Witch."

At least she didn't call me Death Bringer. That one would've embarrassed me under the circumstances.

"But I've done terrible things," I whispered.

"And you will more than make up for them. That much I can see."

There were so many questions I wanted to ask, but they seemed to disappear into the black hole of my mind. I was too overwhelmed to think straight.

"One last thing before you go." She dipped a hand into the folds of her robe and removed a gold chain with a red stone attached to it. "This amulet will keep you safe on your return journey. Even portals are not impervious to the dangers here."

I ducked as the necklace passed over my head and came

to rest around my neck. I looked down to admire the deep red amulet.

"I don't know how to repay you for your kindness," I said.

"It is not I you will repay."

I suddenly remembered the book. I didn't want to start a war between Houses by leaving it behind. Prince Maeron made it very clear how important the book was to House Lewis.

"If you don't mind," I began.

The goddess knew what the request would be. She placed the book in my outstretched hands. "Your friend is doing a valiant job of keeping the portal open, but her magic wanes in this realm. You must go now."

She didn't need to tell me twice. Tucking the book under my arm, I turned and bolted up the steps of the amphitheater and past the judgmental gazes of the...judges. The golden gates parted as I approached and I kept running —to the brave knight who was waiting for me. To Liam and Alaric. To George. Hope filled my heart as I ran straight through the portal.

The world was still blanketed in darkness, but at least it would continue to exist.

Chapter Sixteen

L ondon and I emerged from Central Park drenched in a mixture of sweat, swamp, and water. In other words, we were disgusting. I was relieved to see the rest of our party gathered on the sidewalk. They made it back safely. I quickly counted heads to be sure. Everyone was present and accounted for. I noticed George perched on top of a lamppost. The phoenix flew down to greet me.

Knights moved aside as Alaric moved with preternatural speed to engulf me in his arms. "Thank the gods. I was ready to come for you myself."

"He was," Liam chimed in. "One more minute and I would've been king."

London cleared her throat. "I hate to interrupt the royal succession discussion, but is there somewhere we can clean off?" She touched her head with trepidation. "I'm fairly certain there's a small bird nesting in my hair."

Alaric kissed the top of my head. "Let's go back to the compound and get you checked out."

"No checking required. I'm fine," I insisted. "A shower and a hot meal before I hit the road and I'll be right as rain."

I didn't miss the glimmer of sadness in the vampire king's eyes. "I was hoping your trip to the netherworld might change your mind."

A caravan of armored trucks arrived outside the park.

"Finally," Liam said. "How long ago did you call for transport, Your Majesty?"

Ignoring him, Alaric opened the door of the first vehicle and gestured to me. "Your carriage awaits, milady."

We rode together in the back of the truck where his hand found mine. "Thank you for everything."

"You don't have to thank me."

"What happened in there?"

I shook my head. "You don't want to know."

"That bad, huh?"

"A hellish nightmare." I snuggled against him. "But worth it."

He stroked my hair. "How can you say a thing like that and still plan to leave?"

I tilted back my head to look at him. "Because nothing's changed. You're still a vampire king and I'm still a blood witch." I planted a firm kiss on his lips. "It would be the fast track to the end of our relationship, and I don't want that."

"No, *this* is the fast track to end our relationship. You're not even willing to try to make it work. That's not like you, Britt."

"There's too much at stake now," I explained. "I had nothing to lose before..."

"Before what?" he prompted.

"Before you," I whispered.

The truck slowed to a stop and the back door opened. "Your Majesty," the driver said.

Alaric squeezed my hand and exited the vehicle. "Olis

will want to debrief you once you get cleaned up. Why don't we meet up afterward?"

I gave him a long look. I knew if I spent one more night with Alaric that I'd never leave. I had to give myself this chance to prove I was more than a king's consort. More than an outcast witch. I had to atone for my sins or I'd end up like Set. "I think it would be better if we didn't, Your Majesty." I looked away before I could see his pained expression.

London joined me inside the compound. "I understand there's a debriefing in an hour."

I nodded. "Just enough time to shower and eat."

"I'm a vegetarian," London said. "Will that be a problem?"

"For you?" I snorted. "You're a hero. Nothing will be too much trouble."

Doors opened and closed for us. Clean clothes were delivered, along with soap and fresh towels. The meal was sumptuous. London, Liam, and I ate with her companions in the dining hall. I was envious of their camaraderie. I had that with Liam and even Alaric to a certain extent, but I'd never had that with other women. It was hard to see witches as anything other than the group that cast me aside—but thanks to the knights, I was learning to view them more charitably.

"Why don't we have knights?" Liam asked. "I feel like we're missing out."

"Because this is New York," Davina said, as though that answered the question.

"How many of you are there?" I asked.

"Two more in our order. Minka and Neera stayed behind at the Circus to hold down the fort," Briar said.

Liam's brow creased. "You're part of a circus? Interesting."

"We should really be getting back," Ione said. "My sister will certainly be fed up with Minka by now."

"London, would you do the honors?" Davina asked.

"I can send you all now, but I need to stay for the debriefing."

The guests vacated the table and followed London to a corner of the room where she prepared the portal. Her movements were elegant and precise, like she was conducting an orchestra that played only for her ears.

"You're lucky I don't need to perform a whole ritual like I used to," London said. "Practice makes perfect."

"We really appreciate the support," I told them. "So much better than just sending the book."

"My brother said it was a matter of life and death that affected our Houses," Davina said. "He knows how much I enjoy a good fate-of-the-world scenario." She held out her hand. "I'll need that book now, please. Maeron will never forgive me if I leave it behind. I'll be getting overdue notices for the rest of my immortal life."

I handed over the book as the portal opened. The knights filed through one at a time, along with Davina.

"See you soon," London said.

Davina blew her a kiss as the portal closed behind them.

Liam left the compound to sleep "for a thousand years" as he put it. George accompanied him to make sure he didn't fall asleep en route. Alaric was in a meeting with advisers, which was for the best. I'd talk to Olis, finish packing, and hit the road with George. No awkward goodbyes or backward glances.

Olis met with us in his office at the far end of the compound. I'd been here many times, usually due to a behavior-related infraction.

"Olis, I'd like you to meet London Hayes of the Knights of Boudica."

"So I've heard. It's an honor to make your acquaintance." He bowed. "What's the appropriate title for King Callan's consort?"

I stared at London. "You're the consort of a vampire king?"

"Yes, she is." Olis shot me a pointed look, which was unnecessary. I grasped the comparison.

London smiled. "I told you at the gates that your king would be far better off with you than without you. I know that firsthand."

I let the information wash over me. "And you make it work?"

"We do."

"You can compare relationship notes later," Olis said. "First let us drink to your impressive victory." The wizard poured a rich, purple liquid into two glasses. "House August thanks you for your service."

"We're grateful to you, too. A resurrected god of darkness and evil would've been bad for everybody," London said.

I raised the glass to my nose and inhaled the sweet aroma. "What kind of wine is this?"

"It's called port. It was popular before the Great Eruption."

I tasted the rich alcohol. "Where've you been hiding this stash, Olis?"

"I've been saving it for a special occasion."

"Aw, that's so nice. I don't feel worthy."

He smiled at me. A rare gesture. "Trust me, Britt. You most definitely are."

I clinked London's glass and sampled more. London tipped back her glass and drank.

"Very smooth," London said. "Reminds me of a bottle of..." She paused, her brow furrowing.

"Reminds you of what?" I prompted.

"I forget," she said vaguely. As she took another sip, her eyelids began to close.

I realized my own eyelids felt heavy. Suddenly my whole body felt like a sack of flour. "Olis?" I croaked.

The wizard looked at me, his face impassive. "They never should've tried to break the ward in the park."

"I think we established that."

"I warned them to stop their shenanigans—that they were interfering with my plans, but they refused to listen." He shook his head. "Not everyone is cut out for leadership."

"Truth," I said, although I had no idea why he was bringing this up now.

Olis met my sleepy gaze. "I would tell you I'm sorry for what's about to happen, but the fate of the world outweighs any attachments we may have."

I frowned at him. "You're not making sense. And why are there two of you? Is that a spell?" I poked my finger at the air where a second Olis stood beside the first one.

"All will become clear soon enough," he said.

The glass slid from my fingers and crashed on the floor. Purple liquid pooled between us.

London's movements were languid as she bent to retrieve the broken shards for me. Her own glass slipped from her hand and she crumpled to the floor.

"What's happening?" I asked.

No one answered. I wasn't even certain I'd actually spoken. The world seemed to move in slow motion as my body drifted to the floor to join London's. I reached for her hand and missed. My head hit the flagstone floor and the world faded away.

I felt an urgent hand shaking me awake. My eyes blinked open and I saw London's face hovering above mine.

"Took you long enough, Sleeping Beauty. We have a situation."

I pulled myself to a seated position. "I feel sick to my stomach."

"You're going to feel even worse in a second."

Alarm shot through me. "What happened?"

"Your friend happened."

My friend? It took me a second to realize she meant Olis. The wizard was the last person I'd seen before—this.

"Olis isn't my friend." Although I didn't consider him my enemy—until now. "It was the port, right? He drugged us."

"And somehow managed to transport us out of the compound."

My whole body stiffened. "Where are we?"

"I don't know. It's not the city, I can tell you that much."

Olis snuck us out of the city? That wily bastard. All that talk about trusting him had been a ruse. It seemed the silver-tongued wizard had finally gone full traitor.

"You're close to the king. Will you be missed?" London asked.

I groaned. "Normally I'd say yes, except he knows I was planning to leave the city. I only stayed because of the crisis."

Alaric wouldn't think to check my apartment and see the suitcase still there—or maybe he would. Either way, George would alert him to my absence. Alaric knew I'd never leave the phoenix behind. Either way I wasn't a damsel in distress awaiting my savior. Whatever the situation was, London and I could handle it—I hoped.

"The knights will know something's wrong when I don't return. They'll tell Callan."

"Great, and that will spark a war between Houses. You were taken from the compound. They won't believe Alaric is innocent."

"We can't worry about them. Right now, we have to worry about us." She moved to the window and tapped the glass. "I can sense the ward all around us. Feels like the work of an entire coven."

I tried to get my bearings as I struggled to my feet. "What can you see?"

"There's a bit of light, but nothing that tells me where we are."

"You're a portal witch, aren't you? Can't you...?"

She shook her head, cutting off my question. "The ward is blocking my magic, too. Whoever they are, they knew enough about us to take precautions."

I pressed my face to the glass and peered outside. Silhouettes of trees lined the background like a fortress. A queasy feeling started in the pit of my stomach and quickly began to spread to the rest of me.

London must've sensed my unease because she asked in a quiet voice, "What do you see?"

"Nothing good."

Two female cardinals took flight, no doubt to spread the word of our capture.

And they say you can't go home again.

Preorder Glass King to find out how the trilogy ends!

Printed in Great Britain
by Amazon